Arabesques

BOOKS BY SERHIY ZHADAN
IN ENGLISH TRANSLATION

Arabesques: New Stories
How Fire Descends: New and Selected Poems
Sky Above Kharkiv: Dispatches from the Ukrainian Front
A Harvest Truce: A Play
The Orphanage: A Novel
A New Orthography: Poems
What We Live For, What We Die For: Selected Poems
Mesopotamia
Voroshilovgrad
Depeche Mode

SERHIY ZHADAN

Arabesques

NEW STORIES

Translated from the Ukrainian
by Isaac Stackhouse Wheeler

A MARGELLOS
WORLD REPUBLIC OF LETTERS BOOK

Yale UNIVERSITY PRESS | NEW HAVEN & LONDON

The Margellos World Republic of Letters is dedicated to making literary works from around the globe available in English through translation. It brings to the English-speaking world the work of leading poets, novelists, essayists, philosophers, and playwrights from Europe, Latin America, Africa, Asia, and the Middle East to stimulate international discourse and creative exchange.

Originally published as Арабески. Нові оповідання by Meridian Czernowitz,

Yale University Press books may be purchased in quantity for educational, business, or promotional use. For information, please e-mail sales.press@yale.edu (U.S. office) or sales@yaleup.co.uk (U.K. office).

Set in Source Serif type by Motto Publishing Services.
Printed in the United States of America.

Library of Congress Control Number: 2025940601
ISBN 978-0-300-28434-8 (paper)

A catalogue record for this book is available from the British Library.

Authorized Representative in the EU: Easy Access System Europe, Mustamäe tee 50, 10621 Tallinn, Estonia, gpsr.requests@easproject.com.

10 9 8 7 6 5 4 3 2 1

Contents

Arabesques

Beckon Me to the Gate

On March 2nd—day seven of the war—Kolia called and asked him to pick up a body. Artem wasn't surprised. He did ask for clarification, though. "Whose exactly?"

"My mom's neighbor's," Kolia said. "Hasn't left the apartment in seven days. They got hit. There's hardly anyone left in the whole building. Just a guy on the first floor looking after a bunch of cats, uh, and my mom's neighbor—this old lady. I gave the guy a call. 'She hasn't come out in seven days, won't open the door, hasn't made a sound.' That's what he told me. There's shelling over there, the police won't go. Gotta get the body, though, because it'll start to smell once the days get warmer."

"What if she's still alive?" Artem inquired.

"All the more reason to go get her."

On day one, as soon as the shelling started, Kolia and his mom had left the city and gone away somewhere. He didn't tell anyone where they were staying. He did call everyone and give them assignments, though: drive over there, find this or that person, deliver something here. He personally didn't want to return—his mom wouldn't let him go, which was much appreciated.

It was evening. Artem called his buddy Goner. The two of

them had been doing this for about a week, getting people out of the besieged city.

"We have to get an old lady out tomorrow," Artem said.

"Does she have a lot of stuff?" Goner inquired.

"Don't think so."

"Can she walk?" Goner persisted.

"Can't say for sure."

"Any broken bones?"

"Are you plannin' on marrying her or something?" Artem asked, exasperated.

He lay down on the floor. That's where he slept. For some reason, he was under the illusion that the floor was safer. The windows above him loomed darkly, as did the rest of them, all through the building. Nobody in the city turned their lights on after dark. He was sleeping in the hull of a ship whose crew had gone ashore a week ago and not returned. All week the city lay like an animal with a snapped spine—you're both itching to help and scared to come close. All week, residents were making their way out of the city. Few people remained out on the streets; suddenly, the sparse streets became vast, empty, and tender. Like after a pogrom.

He slept poorly, didn't have any dreams. He was actually glad to wake up. Goner called at eight and said he was outside. Artem came out of his apartment building and surveyed the deserted street. He hopped into their van, said "Hello," and they got going. They each relayed what news they had as they rode. None of it was good. They stopped talking. They passed through the empty city center, spotted a few cars with soldiers in them at several intersections, whipped over the bridge, crossed a large avenue, and drove into a jumble of single-family homes, winding toward the ring road. There there stopped. There was a field a ways off, beyond a white wall of prefab apartment blocks. To the left, behind several fences and poplar trees, a few older five-story apartment buildings loomed red. One of them was theirs.

They avoided a pothole, slowly slid down a side street strewn with crushed brick, went around a looted kiosk, and drove up to the first building.

"What's the number of this building?" Artem asked, to himself more than anyone else.

"God only knows."

"Have to ask someone."

"Who?"

They got out and stood by the building, listening intently. It was so quiet inside, like somebody was eavesdropping. They didn't want to go in. It was quiet outside, too. The neighborhood hadn't gotten hit that day.

"Look," Goner said with a nod.

A bit farther away, on the other side of the building, a man stood. In his forties. Track jacket, ski hat, and glasses. He stood, silent, surveying. A dog, a German shepherd, sat under a tree nearby.

"Is this building number 5?" Artem shouted to him.

The man remained silent.

"Why isn't he saying anything?" Artem asked Goner quietly.

"He's afraid."

"Of who?"

"Me," Goner explained, heading forward.

Artem followed him.

They approached the man. He kept silent, hiding his hands in his jacket pockets and looking off to the side. His gaze was unseeing—it was as if he couldn't see anything or, actually, he just didn't like what he saw. The dog gave all three of them a squeamish look.

"Hey, do you live here?" Goner asked.

The man nodded, adjusting his glasses.

"Is this building number 5?"

The man nodded again.

"Then why didn't you say so?" Goner asked, getting riled up.

"Do you live here?" Artem asked.

"Yeah, I do. I live in this building." Turns out the man could speak.

"Do you know Kolia?"

"I do," the man said. "I was born here, in this building. And I came back here after I got divorced. Now I live alone."

"That's good," Artem answered. "I mean that you know Kolia. He asked us to check up on an elderly lady. In this building. He said that she hasn't come out of her apartment for the past few days. You know her?"

"I do."

"Has she come out of her apartment?" Goner asked.

"She hasn't."

"Show us the way," Artem said, and let the man go ahead.

The building was dank and empty, like a store in a small village. There were old chairs on the landings.

"Is she resting?" Artem asked the man.

"Yeah. She used to come out every day. I helped her when I could. I hardly have any time, though. Work."

They stopped talking. They walked up to the fifth floor. The door was upholstered in brown artificial leather. The leather was all cut up, like someone had gone after it with a kitchen knife. They rang the doorbell, knocked for a long time, then listened intently to the silence. They'd have to break in.

"Does she have anyone?" Artem asked. "Kids, grandkids?"

"A grandson," the man replied. "In Russia."

"Bust it open." Artem stepped back, letting Goner come forward.

Goner kicked the door, and it flew open. They stepped inside and stood in the entryway. Artem realized that all three of them had subconsciously detected a smell. Books. Old books. And old books smell no better than old people. Especially unread ones. They smell of poverty. They smell like love that is meager, inadequate. They walked into the main room and saw a couch covered by a blanket, a dead black TV, and shelves' worth of literature.

"Was she a librarian?" Goner asked.

"A teacher," said the man. "She read a lot. I love reading, too."

"Good for you," Goner replied, and headed toward the smaller room.

The old lady lay on her bed. She wore a warm sweatsuit and wool socks, a kerchief wrapped around her lower back. Before she died, she may have been chilly. She had sharp facial features, seemingly etched with a pencil; the opening of her mouth stood out darkly, like it had been transcribed with coal on gray paper. A comb had fallen out of her gray hair, and it lay on the pillow. Arms tranquilly stretched out along the body. Generally speaking, she had a calm look to her. Like she'd grown cold, then calmed down, and then died.

Artem thought that in homes where dead people lie there's always enough room for everyone, they're always spacious. Possibly because nobody's making a fuss, nobody's goofing around; nobody's living their regular life, which always makes more room for turmoil than logic. He also thought back to when his mom died—still so young, yet downtrodden and doomed—to when he, a first grader, was picked up early from school. It was the beginning of fall; women walked him down the street, holding his hand, and shed showy tears. More than anything else he'd wanted to break free so he wouldn't be shepherded along like a child. And he was shown his mom like a child would be—here, take a look at her, this dead woman who looks nothing like herself, with black circles under her eyes, wearing a dark, formal outfit, one she had worn once before for someone's wedding, if at all—this is your mom, look at her, remember her this way. What he remembered most of all was being ashamed of the adults who were not capable of being honest and sincere, who turned everything into an act of buffoonery and a poor performance, who stood around him, keeping him from averting his eyes, turning around, and leaving. What he wanted most, at that moment, was to leave and go to his room—just to sit there and not think about anything. Not think about school, where he would be bullied the following day, once again, not think about his dad, whom he hadn't seen for over a year and who probably wouldn't be coming that day either; not think about the awful smells coming from the kitchen, where dinner was being cooked for the women who had come to prepare the deceased for burial. So he had to stand there and try to commit his dead mom to memory and see the women's depleted hands, red from washing the dishes and the floor, as his gaze caught the mirror, shrouded in black, which could not reflect either his despair or his dry eyes or his desire to grow up as quickly as possible, to be an adult already, and have a key he could use to lock himself inside his own home.

"I have a library, too," the man said, addressing not so

much Artem and Goner as the deceased. "I have a nice library."

"What year was she born?" Goner interrupted him.

"'45."

"She's a child of war," Goner said.

"Yeah, a child of war," the man concurred.

"A child of war," Artem repeated in his head. "She was born during a war and died during a war. She gathered a library of books in between. And taught her students something, talked to her neighbors about something, loved her grandson, fell asleep in a sweatsuit and didn't wake up."

"Look for her papers in the cabinet," he told Goner. "So they can file everything properly."

Goner opened the top doors of the cabinet and did, indeed, see a bundle of documents and photographs.

"We're taking her papers with us," Artem told the man. "And then we'll give them to Kolia. Keep an eye on the apartment."

"But I have work," the man objected.

"That's all right." Artem had stopped listening. "You should get going. Your dog's waiting for you."

They retrieved the blanket from the larger room, spread it out on the floor, placed the old lady on it, and carried her outside. Then they loaded her into the van and beeped a farewell at the man.

Artem drove this time. He attentively navigated the potholes, tuning in to the morning silence. Goner sat next to him, taking the photographs out of the bundle, glancing at them inattentively, and then tucking them back inside. He lingered on one of them. Artem ran his eyes over it, too. The girl in the photo was so young and so poor. A simple dress, not something you'd wear to a formal event. Inconspicuous shoes. She stood somewhere in the street; behind her, a plain brick wall, a window, and an open gate were visible. That's all—no sign of the time the picture was taken, no details, nothing to latch on to except her, except the look in her eyes.

The photo was dim and faded, like she was standing there in the early twilight. Standing and looking from the past into the future. In the future, there was a long life filled equally with good and evil. The future held lots of unread literature. The future held death.

The Light Will Rise Above the City of the Righteous

"What's his name?"

"Serhiy. I think."

"Do you know him?" Vovchyk asks.

"Misha vouched for him," Valera replies. "That's all I know."

"Well, if he vouched for him . . . But why here? Couldn't we talk in the office?"

"Doing it here will put us at ease—and him, too," Valera explains.

"Then let's get a move on. I wanna go home."

"All right then."

Fall is just beginning. If you sit here in the office kitchen, on the tenth floor, and look down at the city, it may appear as though it's still summertime on the streets: lazy passersby, slow streetcars, and an endless evening that leisurely and inexorably imbues everything with ample red light. Early evenings continue to enchant with their tranquillity; time's touch is akin to tree bark—warmed by the summer, infused with sun. When you're thirty, it's nice to look at the city from above, it's nice to see the distant broken line of the horizon, it's nice to have a good job. And a place where you can hide from that job.

Back in the spring, they'd ordered simple, comfortable

chairs instead of plastic ones, so they'd want to stick around. They don't really have anywhere to rush off to; as well-educated thirty-year-olds, they're doing all right for themselves. Valera, tall, skinny, and sporting a red beard, looks like a tourist who is unsure of where to go. Vovchyk, as round as a ball, wears work pants with a dozen pockets and a Bowie T-shirt. They don't look like millionaires. But they are. Valera approaches the kitchen shelves, takes out a case of mineral water, rips a bottle out of the plastic like it's an exotic fruit, plops down on a chair, and takes a sip. Vovchyk reads the news on his phone.

He arrives right on time, at five-thirty, following Larysa into the kitchen. She takes him by the elbow and lets him go ahead. "Am I excused now?" her eyes ask. There's plenty of light in the room, which makes it feel cozy and calm.

"Hi!" Vovchyk says cheerfully.

"Hey there," Valera says kindly. "Take a seat wherever," he adds, and falls silent.

The man moves toward a chair, sits down tentatively. The sun's evening rays beat down on them. The kitchen is a translucent riverbank with a silty bottom.

"Tea? Coffee?" Valera asks.

"What are you drinking?" he asks in reply.

"Water," Valera answers, flustered, and nods at the bottle. "Want some?"

"Sure," he says.

"Let's use the informal 'you.'" Valera walks over, plucks another bottle out of the case, opens it, and hands it to him.

"I'm Vovchyk. And this is Valera."

"Serhiy Stanislavovych Ponomariov," says the man, giving them his full name, patronymic included.

"So formal," Vovchyk chuckles.

Valera smiles, albeit somewhat sheepishly. Serhiy Stanislavovych laughs, too.

"Okay, then," Vovchyk says casually, deliberately so. "Serhiy Stanislavovych. Misha vouched for you, so this is pretty much just a formality, but we wanted to have a little chat with you. Don't worry. It's cool, all right?"

"Got it," Serhiy Stanislavovych answers flatly. "Misha told me you're friends. I just don't want you to take me on because of that. Know what I mean?"

Vovchyk glances at Valera and notices that he has tensed up.

"It's all good," Vovchyk says, carefully choosing his words; "you really are a good fit."

"Hey," Serhiy Stanislavovych interrupts him delicately and lowers his head, like he's peeking at a cheat sheet. "Can I say something?"

"Uh, sure," Vovchyk agrees, somewhat puzzled, and once again glances at Valera, whose eyes wander around the room, seemingly trying to latch on to something.

They remain silent for some time. A room soaking in sunlight, a floor flooded with warmth. Evening encroaches, emerging in little nooks and shadows.

"If only I could go outside," Vovchyk thinks, "and get away from all this."

"Look, you . . ." Serhiy Stanislavovych begins again. It's unclear who he's addressing. "I mean, I appreciate that you two agreed to all of this, that you found the time, that you're listening to me."

"It's all good," Vovchyk says, trying to encourage him.

"Nah, it's just . . . Can I say something?"

"Sure, sorry." Finally, Vovchyk decides not to interrupt

him; he kicks back in his chair and wearily shuts his eyes. It grows dark and disconcerting.

"Thanks." Serhiy Stanislavovych pauses and then continues. "It's really important to me that you don't think of Misha right away when you look at me, that you see me for who I really am."

Finally, Valera looks at him attentively. He's in his late thirties, older than they are, and this immediately catches his eye. Valera's, that is. He sits there in his black suit. He buttoned his shirt unevenly, but he doesn't seem to have noticed. Valera wants to walk over and adjust those damn buttons, but he restrains himself, instead examining them like they're something truly important. Serhiy Stanislavovych grows anxious, though, not knowing where to put his big, dark hands, realizing that everyone is looking at his hands, and trying to hide them like slabs of dark, dead meat brought back from the market.

"I used to have a job in my field," Serhiy Stanislavovych says. "I'm here for a reason."

"Sounds good," Valera suddenly speaks up. "Let's cut to the chase, then. Are you aware of the sheer volume of work involved and how much you'll have to do?"

A pigeon clumsily lands on the windowsill, peers into the room, sees three strange grown men, and with its bird's eye perceives a whole world of human relationships and mysteries, a marvelous world chock-full of a thousand tiny details, which one can examine and explore endlessly.

"I am," Serhiy Stanislavovych says calmly. "I think it'll be a bit tough at first, but I'll manage."

"You sure?" Valera asks.

"Yeah," Serhiy Stanislavovych replies just as calmly.

"You've got a serious operation here. But I've seen it all," he says with a laugh.

They think about laughing in reply yet hold themselves back. Vovchyk automatically takes out his phone and glances at something on his screen, like he's here by himself. Valera sets his bottle aside, rises, approaches the window. Down below, the trees cast deep, heavy shadows—there's no discerning what hides there. Yet if you look closely, you can distinctly make out the wind grazing blades of grass, picking up, brushing against leafy crowns, turning inside out above the buildings, and enveloping the entire city, chock-full of light and warmth, blanketed by the sky, and surrounded by the sun and crescent moon. The more you look at it, the more mysteries and hidden chambers reveal themselves, the more voices you hear, and the more motion and joy you feel.

Shadows grow deeper, twilight sets in. Vovchyk rises and switches on the light. Serhiy Stanislavovych realizes that he's holding everyone up, but he wants to make one last point before parting.

"I can do it," he says. "Nobody promised us that life would be easy. Nobody promised me, that's for sure. And even if they had, I wouldn't have believed them."

"Okay," Valera responds. "You'll be a good fit, then."

"We'll see," Serhiy Stanislavovych replies.

"You can find your own way out?"

"Of course."

He leaves. They sit in the kitchen for a long time. Valera produces a bottle of wine and uncorks it. Then another. Vovchyk talks about his daughter, about her new school and her new teachers, says that his little girl is happy there, and that she's a good student. He keeps talking and suddenly feels that he doesn't want to go anywhere, that he doesn't want to leave, that he feels the most secure here, in this kitchen, under these yellow ceiling lights. Valera talks about his kids, too, brags about them, too: competitions, medals, the national team. They sit there, bragging about their kids, getting gradually drunk. It gets very dark.

"Hey," Vovchyk interjects, unable to contain himself. "But how is he supposed to do the job? I mean, he's blind."

"It's not like we're asking him to paint portraits," Valera objects harshly. "He'll do fine. You'll ask the folks in the office to help him out for the first few days."

"What happened to him?"

"Mine. Misha told me that their pickup hit a mine. Outside Kharkiv. They took a wrong turn when they were heading back. They all got blown up, the whole group, but Serhiy Stanislavovych survived somehow. Now he can't see anything, though. All right, let's get going."

Valera rises, collects the empty bottles, and washes the glasses—doesn't like leaving them for the cleaning lady. Vovchyk abruptly finishes reading the news, yet stays put. Valera tosses him his jacket and gives him an inquisitive look.

"You coming?" he asks.

"I'm gonna stay here a little longer," Vovchyk says, shaking his head. "You can get going, though."

"All right," Valera says, patting him on the back. "See you tomorrow."

He holds the door open as he's about to leave.

"Don't forget to turn the lights out."

Victory

RIP IT OUT LIKE YOUR ENEMY'S HEART

"Wait, how old are you again?" Bohdan asks. "Eleven?"

"Twelve," Tokha corrects him. "Did you forget?"

"This whole thing feels like one long day," Bohdan says, offering an excuse. "Don't be mad."

"Fine." Tokha is no longer listening.

They step outside into the June afternoon sun, instantly blinded. Their apartment building is old and sturdy, tucked between wide walkways and heavy trees. The city center is a bit farther away, beyond the river. It's quiet here—single-family homes, summer greenery. You can pass through a fence gate and go missing, never to be found. There are robust, red-brick homes, a road paved with crushed shingles, and a streetcar track overrun by grass this summer like a river nobody swims in anymore.

"Ready to roll?" Bohdan asks.

"Sure," Tokha replies and walks ahead.

Past some linden trees, they duck under an arch and enter the neighboring courtyard. On a bench outside an apartment building, women warily warm themselves, looking somehow self-conscious. They spot Bohdan, fall silent, and then greet him tentatively. Clearly, they don't know how to greet guys like him, so different from themselves, brusque and so large. Bohdan greets them in reply, places his hand on Tokha's shoulder, tugs him through a hole in the fence and into the schoolyard. They pass a playground, skirt the school, and emerge on one of the main avenues.

"Look." Tokha stops and points at the building opposite them. "You see that?"

"Yeah." Confounded, Bohdan contemplates the black, burnt-out box of the university. "Aren't they going to rebuild it?"

"Dunno," Tokha answers, and quickly crosses the avenue.

The dusty fishbowl of the metro station, the empty little square, the gray structure of the House of Culture behind some trees. Bohdan hasn't been here since early March. That was ages ago. "In the summer, you feel like living here," he thought to himself. The winters here, though, are like waking up at a train station every morning, without a ticket, without any of your things or any hope you'll be able to go anywhere.

Summer has just begun, and vendors run around Kharkiv's half-empty market in a businesslike fashion, and there's hardly anyone around, and nobody haggles, nobody sulks. And they walk down the chilly market rows to the bus station as the cumbersome construction of the stadium comes into view. They plod along the chain-link fence, pass through the gate, reach the practice fields, sit down in plastic chairs, dark from dust and downpours, and eye the artificial turf in silence.

Bohdan feels out of sorts in his regular clothes. Yesterday evening, as soon as he'd arrived and taken a shower, he opened his wardrobe right away, began rooting through his clothes, thinking about what to wear. He had a lot of clothes;

they were well-worn and smelled of last winter. In other words, he didn't want to wear them. Eventually, he found a pair of jeans, a T-shirt, and sneakers. His regular clothes should have felt safe and snug. Instead, he felt as though he'd taken them off a dead man. He walked around all day with this, this smell of winter, this smell of burnt asphalt. In the morning, he and Tokha had agreed to go to the stadium, like in the good old days.

"No one's there," Tokha warned him. "Nobody plays anymore."

"Let's just take a look," Bohdan insisted.

So there they sat. Tokha, with his unkempt hair and his sweatsuit, was out of it, like he'd come to see a doctor he hadn't yet learned to fear. And then there was Bohdan in his rumpled clothes and white sneakers, his face burned by the eastern Ukrainian sun and his beard trimmed just yesterday. There really weren't too many people on the fields; on the far one, in the corner, kids ran back and forth, but there weren't enough of them to make two teams, so it would have been hard to call it a game.

"Why aren't you and the guys playing?" Bohdan asks, tentatively, so as not to strike a nerve.

Tokha considers responding with an insulting remark but restrains himself. Bohdan notices this, regrets what he's said, but also restrains himself and waits.

"Everyone just kind of scattered," Tokha says calmly. "Drone, the goalie, remember him? He's in Poland. Sanka left, too. And so did the Kid. Who am I supposed to play with?"

"Yeah . . ." Bohdan says.

The sky is round and as clear as can be. Go ahead, you can be a hero under this sky. Yet there's no one here to be a hero: the fields are empty, everything's quiet, even the supermarket across the street is orphaned and dilapidated. Two women with their dogs. Looks like the dogs are the ones who need a stroll, though; the women remain silent, not saying anything at all.

"I used to love taking you here," Bohdan says. "Especially in the winter. When it's dark and the floodlights are on, and everyone's shouting, and you can see their breath. Remember that?"

"Yeah," Tokha replies. "Honestly, I was afraid whenever you came to watch, afraid to lose. That's why I'd play so badly. I was nervous."

"For real?" Bohdan asks, bewildered.

"For real. Seemed like you wanted to win more than I did."

"Well, players take the field to win, don't they?"

"Maybe," Tokha replies reluctantly, and looks at the empty field. "I guess? I mean I've never won anything."

"You will one day."

"Doubt it. I kept playing soccer because I didn't want to hurt your feelings."

"Nah," Bohdan says incredulously. "You liked it, though."

"I liked when it was all over," Tokha admits. "I didn't like anything else. Why play in the first place?"

"What do you mean? To win."

"Okay, then."

Bohdan reaches into his pocket and finds a piece of gum. Fruit-flavored. He wants to give it to Tokha, but he looks at his well-worn sneakers, how they're almost adult-sized, and restrains himself. Then he offers the gum anyway. At first, Tokha holds back, then accepts it once he sees that it's fruit-flavored. They return home in the early evening. At home, they sit in the kitchen, staring at their phones and not saying anything. Tokha realizes that Bohdan's taking it personally, so he cracks first.

"Wanna watch a movie?" he suggests.

"Let's watch some soccer," Bohdan suggests in turn.

"Sure." Tokha doesn't object. "But who's playing tonight?"

"Nobody. Let's find an old game."

"But why? You can just look up the score."

"It's not about the final score. Did you see when Maradona scored with his hand? That's the most famous goal in soccer history."

"Yeah," Tokha says.

"Have you seen the entire game, though?"

"Nah," Tokha says. "Do you actually want to watch it again?"

"Yeah, let's do it."

Bohdan takes out his laptop and searches for the game. They go into the main room and flop down on the couch. A long, leisurely evening sets in outside. It's quiet in their building. It's like time is broken, but nobody is in a hurry to fix it. Tokha watches, somewhat bored. Conversely, Bohdan offers running commentary.

"Here it is, look," he says, pointing. "The attack's starting, you see? There he is. You see?"

"Yep," Tokha says.

"It's coming up. Four minutes into the half," Bohdan continues. "The second goal's coming up. Look."

"Do you get it now?" he asks Tokha some time later.

"No," Tokha replies.

"What don't you get?" Bohdan grows anxious.

"What's the big deal?" Tokha asks. "Scoring with your hand."

"What's the big deal? You really don't get it, do you?"

Bohdan kicks back, starts thinking. Then he sits up abruptly and half-closes the laptop. He stays silent, searches for words. "His feelings are hurt," Tokha thinks, regretting he started all this.

"Know why he's great? Because he won. He won, get it? Winners are forgiven a lot. Not everything, but a lot, that's for sure. Victory . . . it disarms you. Since you look at whoever won and you start to understand what he was willing to do. What was he willing to do? Well, anything really. To go out there and rip that damn victory out like a heart out of someone's chest. Doesn't matter if it's with your hand, your teeth, your head, or your fingernails. Take a look at him now, after it's all over. What questions could you have for him? Just go out there and do what needs to be done. Without leaving the enemy a single chance. Without listening to anyone, without believing anyone, without making any excuses. Go and rip it out. Like a heart. Like a fish out of a river. That's it. Then let everyone ask their questions, let them get offended. Victories can't be overruled. A loss can be explained, but there's generally nothing to be done about it. Got it?"

"Yeah," Tokha says somberly. "When are you leaving tomorrow?"

"In the morning."

"Can't you stay?"

"No. They're expecting me."

After that, they watch a movie, talk about this and that, call Tokha's mom, call his grandpa, Bohdan's dad. Tokha tells them about his day and wishes them good night. Then they make their beds, remaining silent. Bohdan peels off his T-shirt and jeans and stuffs them in the washer. He places his clothes by his bed. Although they've been washed, they still smell like weaponry.

“What’s tomorrow looking like for you?” Bohdan asks Tokha.

“Dunno,” he says. “I’ll head downtown.”

“Ah. Text me, all right?”

“Okay.”

“I may not have service. I’ll give you a call when I do.”

“Sounds good.”

“Text me anyway.”

“Sure.”

“Even if you don’t have service.”

“Will do.”

“I love you.”

“Love you too.”

Then the Lord Will Call the Woman

And then a warm early spring came, as if nothing had happened.

We stand under the vast sky, not speaking, and listening to the silence of the outskirts. It's as quiet as an apartment building after a large, feuding family has moved out. Sunday morning, solitary streets on the other side of the fence. The streetcar tracks are rusty after the winter. The streetcars haven't been running since the end of February. Up above, birds break through, spill out of the sky like apples from a pocket, spot our mute crew down below, rise apprehensively back up into the sky, and fly toward the river. We take a minute to warm up and think to ourselves that the birds are now returning, spring is returning, that this peculiar life is continuing, pulling us along like the current pulls the shoes of drowning victims. It's on these days, when time freezes like a sunbeam on the blade of a knife, that there's one careless movement, one imprudent push, and the light shifts, and after that, an entire city with its hills, tracks, and birds begins to shift, and nothing can halt the advance of warm currents of air, the motion of hot clouds and scorching sun. For now, this brief, nearly imperceptible period of equilibrium persists, when winter backs away from you like a dog that trusts you, yet remains at arm's length, and waits to see if you'll call it or not. The wind picks up, the air gets really warm, everyone faces the sun—it's nice out in the sun, and you just want to stand stock-still. Stand there and feel life going on, mercilessly and gently. But then we're called over. We turn around, put our phones on silent, and head into the church.

The church is cramped; it smells of clothes worn close to a bonfire and men who've been on the road. Many people came straight to the churchyard, driving down battered roads all night, afraid they wouldn't make it on time. Men, primarily soldiers, somewhat tentatively crowd around by the exit, just in case, like schoolboys who have forgotten to do their homework and are hoping that their teacher won't notice them. Most of them aren't quite sure how to act in a church, so they behave courteously, just in case. There aren't many women; they move to the center, closer to the priest. I spot Dina right away.

"Look," I say to my crew. "Dina made it."

"Someone drove her here last night," one of our guys replies. "She didn't bring the kid."

Dina stands amid the group of women; the women encircle her, seemingly protecting her from something, whispering something to her, handing her something, touching and hugging her. The priest stands in the middle of the church, eyeing the damp, taciturn crowd, staring intently, as though he's trying to figure out who's in charge. Eventually, he turns toward Dina, approaches her, and says something to her in a compelling whisper, a whisper that elicits trust. Dina agrees. What else can she do?

The priest is lean and wears glasses that make him look a little too professorial. When he reads the Scriptures, it sounds as though he's quoting himself. He isn't quite sure how to behave around these servicemen, whose boots still have blood on them. He walks around and tells them what they can and cannot touch like they're children at a museum. Occasionally, he glances back at the casket, at the deceased.

The deceased is eyed by everyone. It's as though they want to make sure that it's really him. Those who haven't seen him recently may not recognize him. Sallow face, indistinct features. Like someone has lent a careless hand and touched his face. Combed-back hair, touched-up wrinkles. Dark, heavy hands on his chest. And a trace of his wedding ring on his dead finger.

The men give him inquisitive looks, as they have in the past; they continue to feel like they're his subordinates, they continue to view him as their commander. Yet the women look at him with pity, the way they typically look at the deceased, that is. They all greet each other, although many of them haven't met before. Death brings them together somehow. Death is like a streetcar now—all that matters is where you're supposed to get off, not how you got on.

At first, I think about pushing my way toward the front, closer to Dina, greeting the people I know, but then I stop—what am I supposed to do among these women, what am I even supposed to say to them? Here I have to be quiet, be quiet and listen. That's what everyone's doing—being quiet and listening while the priest hands out candles, places them between the men's uncooperative fingers like he's threading branches. After this, he begins singing, and everyone remains quiet, listening. They look around, seeking out people they know. Upon recognizing someone, they nod and then refocus on the priest's voice.

Nobody listens much to the words. Something about mercy and memory. Mercy and memory, something along those lines. This is what he tries to explain, to articulate. So that we can all understand, so that all of this will make some sort of sense. His voice is quiet. Alongside this death, it wanes and wanders. Death is truly vast, casting a cold, heavy shadow and encasing everyone with murk and moisture. And everyone stands, looking at the deceased's sallow face, breathing the air pervaded with melted wax tinged with wet peacoats, thinking about the sun out in the churchyard, on the other side of the wall, about dry grass, about empty streetcar tracks, thinking and not understanding a single thing about mercy—or about memory, for that matter.

The priest also sees that nobody understands what he's saying. Yet he has to speak—the presence of death prescribes something important be said, something self-evident, something which will release the deceased, with his heavy hands, his ribs broken by bullets and hidden under a white blanket. The priest surveys the church and adopts a more probing tone, seeking to elicit trust and primarily addressing the women, who stand nearly on top of the casket, seemingly fearing for it, seemingly engaged in a dispute over it, as if they intend to take it with them, along with the dead man and the white blanket.

I notice that Dina has changed somehow over the past two months since the last time we saw each other. Like she's receded into the shadows. And the color of her skin—dusky and precious—has suddenly lost all its significance and blended in with the surrounding twilight. Besides this, her dark dress, light coat, and even her glasses, which ought to conceal tears, are all very becoming. Tall, restrained, and resentful—in the presence of death, she looks more compelling. She stands by the casket on the side where his wedding ring once was on his dead hand. She stands there, seemingly reminding everyone that she is entitled to stand right where she is. Nobody takes issue with that. Everyone sympathizes with her.

And the priest starts speaking primarily to her, to Dina, seemingly aware of who needs his words, his hymns, the most. Dina looks at the priest, accepting everything, not objecting at all, seemingly saying, "Fine, let it be mercy, let it be mercy and memory, say everything that needs to be said at these moments." The priest speaks, standing there, so small and despairing between this taciturn woman and vast death, which hovers in the air, applying pressure and breathing heavily, like an animal that had been stalking its wounded prey.

Then she removes her glasses and looks straight ahead; her gaze is dry and dark as charcoal, and nobody is capable of withstanding it. I notice that all the women are crying, crying as they look at the deceased. Dina is the only one not crying; she looks without crying. And this makes things utterly unbearable, makes you want to go outside, out into the sun, makes you want to breathe and speak. I also notice that Dina is looking not at the deceased, not at his sallow face, but off to the side, beyond death, where another woman—skinny, short blond hair—stands in the corner, appearing somewhat detached and disoriented. I recognize her, too. Anna. We don't know each other all that well, but we've seen each other several times in the past few months, since February. Army jacket, no makeup. There she stands, giving Dina the same look, also not turning her gaze away, searing everything around with her green eyes. And nobody appears to take notice; they take no notice of how the women look at each other, how they look around, how darkness thickens around them.

There appears to be a certain similarity between them: the same stillness, resentment, hopelessness. Nevertheless, they're very different. Dina looks at death like a sole heir ought to, with dignity and disdain, and her resentment encompasses all those years, all those years which have been left behind, which she considers her exclusive property, as this is her past, her betrayals and secrets, renunciations and maledictions, and now, right here and now, she'll take them away along with the casket, and the whole story of her life with the deceased, one lasting ten (ten!) years, will finally come to an end, and there won't be anything else—just the shadow of death, just mercy and memory, just two wedding rings on her finger, her own and the deceased's.

Anna, though, looks at all that and harbors despair, attempts to cling to something, anything, in the darkness: to her right to love, to be together without shame, to the brief intimacy of the past few months, such a deep-rooted intimacy. And she thinks that everything that once filled her life has been taken right out of her hands, stripped away since she has no right to any of this: neither to life nor to death, neither mercy nor memory. After all, even her memory will be concealed from everyone for the rest of time—from the melancholy wife of this dead man, from his friends who never wound up becoming her friends, from these women whose names she has no desire to know.

There they stand, recognizing each other, staying silent, not saying anything. They wait until the body can be collected. Yet only Dina realizes that she will be the one to collect the body. Well, actually, Anna knows that, too. She has always known that.

Eventually, the priest falls silent, then issues some instructions to the men. Everyone steps outside, into the fresh air. They take out their phones, check their missed calls. Dina and Anna step away from the crowd, each to her own side, and take out their phones, too. Dina has about two dozen new messages, mostly from common friends—sympathy and support—a call from her kid, a call from the unit. Anna has one missed call from her mom, who's asking her to put money on her phone.

She Is the One to Keep You Warm Through the Night

He didn't like the hotel. It was on a separate floor in a residential building. Cold rooms. Front desk on the first floor, unfriendly women there. Yet women were always unfriendly to him—he should have gotten used to it. They looked at him suspiciously, especially when he took out his wallet and began rooting around in it.

Eventually, she couldn't take it anymore. "Want me to chip in?" she asked. He waved dismissively, a little too abruptly, as if to say, "I got this." She gave him a little "hmm" and stepped away; he paid and took the key. They kept silent as they went up the stairs. There was a certain awkwardness, so they tried to move quickly, running like they were escaping something. She'd arrived before him on purpose, in order to feel more confident—after all, it was her idea, he was the one visiting her, she would be telling him what was what. When they were texting beforehand, he had suggested meeting in the room, but she'd rebuffed him.

"Let's meet outside, near the hotel. Otherwise it could look like something else. You aren't embarrassed, are you?" she asked.

He complied, of course, saying that he had nothing to be embarrassed about, that he just wanted to make things as convenient as possible. After that, he started offering some more explanations. Long story short, their texting ended abruptly. Now she was following him, and she felt how nervous he was; she heard him trying to hold his breath as he walked up the stairs so she—heaven forbid—wouldn't think he was struggling. She's the one who can't keep up, although she left her heavy combat boots with the rest of her gear and put on light sneakers. Nonetheless, everything is heavy, unwieldy, and misplaced. He's in his late twenties—hair cut short, stubble, a black athletic jacket which fits him like he probably asked one of his buddies for some of his civilian clothes instead of wearing his uniform. She's tall, gruff, has short hair—it was dyed a while ago, yet it's still bright.

The room was large and kind of empty. Like some of the furniture had been removed because nobody was using it. A couch with a little table in front of it stood apart. He kept trying to act naturally; this seemed to rattle both of them. Nevertheless, she didn't stop him—let him do what's best for him. He took a bottle of wine out of his backpack and placed it on the table. They stood, looking at the bottle, not knowing what to say.

"The wine may not be any good," he said eventually. "There wasn't anything better."

"No worries," she reassured him.

"Shall we?" he inquired.

"But I don't drink."

"How come?"

"Meds."

"Is it something serious?"

"Uh-huh," she said with a laugh. "I'm mentally unstable. Kidding. Nothing serious, just something to calm my nerves. Keep forgetting to take them, though. So the wine's all yours."

She took a pack of pills out of her pocket, placed them on the bedside table. She thought for a bit, then produced a box of condoms and placed them alongside everything else. He broke into laughter, produced some pills, too, and placed them on the table on the other side of the bed.

"Sleeping pills. I've hardly been able to sleep lately."

"Seems like we're in for a fun night," she replied.

"We'll see. I don't drink wine, though. At all."

"Why'd you get it then?"

"Uh, I thought that's how things are supposed to be."

"Hey." She walks over and takes his hand. "Don't think about how things are supposed to be, all right? Let them be what they'll be. I'm gonna take a shower, and you should take your shoes off. Come on, it's like you're at the train station or something."

"Okay," he said and pulled her toward him. She acquiesced, nuzzling his neck, which made him freeze, stay stock-still, and after he'd stood there like that for a little, she released his hand and went to take a shower.

He kicked off his shoes, fell back onto the bed, took out his phone, checked the news, saw a video of some burnt-out military vehicles, and eventually calmed down.

Once she'd closed the door, she shed her clothes, stepped over them like they were something foreign to her, and then went over to the mirror. She realized that she hadn't seen her own body in a while. They had a shower where her unit was posted, of course, but she frankly lacked a decent mirror in which she could take a look at her whole self. She'd even forgotten when she last stood like this, examining her own reflection. It must have been when she stopped at home for a few days. But, no, that wasn't it. The last time she went home was in the middle of the night, a month ago. She'd slipped into the shower quietly, so as not to wake anyone, tossed her uniform into the washer, reflexively stood under the hot water, stood there a long time and suddenly caught herself thinking that she was standing with her eyes shut, so she wouldn't see anything, wouldn't see the warm towels, the pink robe, the lotions, the shampoos, the loofahs. She could not get herself to look at any of it. She turned off the water, dried off irately, and went to sleep in the kitchen on the couch, where no one else was.

Now she stood in a hotel shower, wet and freezing, in a city near the front lines, one so alien and abhorred by her, in front of a mirror, and she couldn't understand what was irritating her so much. Yes, there was this room: cold, hadn't been cleaned properly, stains on the carpet and a socket ripped out of the wall by the door. Yes, there was the weather: when the dosage of sun is so small, it's as if someone's being stingy with it, when everything's gray and translucent, and there's nothing for your eye to cling to in that translucency. And there was this man, who was all nervous and acting bizarrely, and she started regretting doing this and thinking that all of this was so out of place and ill-timed—their meeting at a gas station in a city she was passing through on her way from the field hospital back to where their unit was posted, his feckless attempt to chat her up, and the fact that she reciprocated and even gave him her name. And the fact that he found her on social media, wrote to her, more cool, more confident, and that she responded to that confidence in an unexpected way and actually replied. And their texting, which immediately went beyond corny jokes and unwarranted constraint. And the fact that she agreed to meet rather quickly (they'd only known each other five days, five frickin' days); she asked her commander for leave, planned everything out, found this damn hotel (there were only two in the city, and she refused to stay at the other one), summoned the courage, and made the trip. She wasn't irritated by any of that, though. So what was it? She looked in the mirror again. Weary body, pale skin, just overall helpless and defenseless. The helplessness, that's what irritated her. She wanted to be strong and self-assured, didn't want to arouse pity and sympathy. Alarm and bewilderment still seeped through her skin—there was no hiding it. And there was that scar by her fractured collarbone—it seemed to have deepened and darkened, like a path through lingering snow. Through snow that should have gone away but hadn't, snow that clung to the spring air, reminded others of itself, of the past, where everything was fractured and shattered, where nothing ought to have remained, yet still did, reminded others of itself through this faded line on her skin. She glanced in the mirror again, wrapped the towel around herself, and went back into the room with him.

He saw her, stood up, wanted to say something, but she didn't let him. Instead, she turned off the light, got into bed, and hugged him. They lay there, kissing for a long time, in a detached way, as if they were just going with the flow, without moving any more than necessary, not hurrying at all, simply floating down the river and feeling the early spring twilight set in, deeper and deeper. Yet when he attempted to unwrap her towel, she stopped him. “Take your time.” He complied, plopped back onto the pillow, and went quiet. They lay there in the darkness, looking silently at the ceiling.

Then she began talking. She told him that she'd been here previously—in this city, that is—several times before all this. She'd graduated from a law school in Kharkiv and worked as an associate at a firm. They did business with one of the major factories here, so her boss kept having her shuttle back and forth to negotiate something or other. He'd take her along when he went, too—he felt more confident with her, and she made him appear more successful. That's how he saw it, at least. Oh, yeah, and he was in love with her. He kept his distance, though, torturing himself and doing all sorts of dumb stuff in the process. Once, during one of their trips, they finally hammered out an agreement. Her boss was decisive and furious, laughing and drinking with his new business partners. That evening, he brought her back to his room and told her that she wouldn't be needing her own room, that she'd be staying with him. Yet they didn't get into a fight or anything; she cracked a few jokes and then started talking about something else. He picked up on that right away, and it kind of took the wind out of his sails, and he collapsed onto the bed. She turned off the light and quietly stepped out. She went down to the lobby, got herself a room, locked herself inside, got undressed, and fell asleep right away. She and her boss returned home the following morning as if nothing had happened.

“I can't stand this city.” She found his hand in the dark. “If someone had told me that I'd come back ten years later, I wouldn't have believed them. And I can't stand hotels either.”

He thought that nobody had ever told him anything like

that about themselves. Women mostly either complained about something or argued with him. This was a kind of serene story; there may not have been much wisdom in it, but at least it wasn't overly emotional or anything. It turned out that people could talk about themselves like this, too. Basically, he could finally take a deep breath, although he was still a little worried about how everything had played out with the wine.

"Things will be what they'll be," he thought. And then her phone lit up.

She had prudently turned off the sound so nobody would disturb her. Yet she reacted to the light. She reluctantly picked up her phone, looked at the screen, and instantly tensed up. Then she tried pulling her hand away.

"What's up?" He, too, was suddenly tense.

"Let go," she said nervously, yanking her hand free and sitting up.

"Did something happen?"

"Everything's fine. Gotta call them back."

"Who?"

"Everything's fine," she repeated, and went back into the bathroom.

He heard her lock the door. She spoke to someone quietly and at length. He grew angry.

"What the hell?" he thought. "She could have told me who it is, at least. What am I even doing here? What's the point of all this? I could be with the crew right now. Our squad has a ton of work to do. The battalion commander didn't want to let me go. He's gonna hassle me tomorrow for bailing on everyone. Better get going and head back now." But then he remembered their texts, what she'd written him, all the thoughtful questions she'd asked him. He thought that hardly anyone had ever taken such an interest in him, especially during the past five years, since he got divorced. Also he thought about her scar, which she appeared to be self-conscious about; he thought of that and decided to stay.

She returned, lay down beside him, and found his hand. He pulled his hand away, lay there, and stayed quiet.

"Sorry," she said eventually. "My daughter called. She's staying with my parents. They got into a fight this morning, so I had to calm her down."

"It's okay." He pulled her toward him again.

"How about getting some sleep? When else will we get the chance . . ."

"All right." He complied right away.

He fell asleep first. Then she did right after him. He didn't get around to taking his pills. Neither did she.

The Minute Hand

He's in his forties. Likes how old he is. He loves talking about himself, and he's started wearing glasses. Whenever he takes them off, he lacks gravitas; it's like he's looking into the void and can't see anything there. That's precisely why he never takes them off. He's arrived in the kind of suit people wear for a special occasion—a birthday party, for instance. Or for a wake. At any rate, he's only got one suit, so he supposes that he'll be buried in it, too. And there's his watch—mechanical, well-worn. He can see the big hand clearly, can't see the little hand all that well, though. So he views time as arbitrary, in a way. The hand's moving—well, okay then. Lean face, short hair. Scar on his chin. That's why he has a beard. Prior to the accident, before the scar, he didn't have a beard. She isn't used to his beard, so she eyes him as she would a stranger. A completely different face, completely different eyes. Everything's different. She hasn't seen him for five years. It isn't just that she's forgotten about him—she's managed to forget how to treat him. And those glasses of his—looks like he took them straight off an older person's face. Uh-huh, and she recognizes his suit right away; she was the one who bought it for him back in the day.

She didn't prepare for his coming in any particular way—just threw on a pair of jeans she typically wore around the house, then a sweater, and pulled her hair back. She considered putting on makeup but then grew angry with herself—the time to put on makeup was five years ago. In general, she tried not to think too much, just wanted to get through this time together—it'd be easier together, and above all, it was the right thing to do. They ought to be together this morning. They hadn't spoken in five years, and that was enough. They were family, after all. You can refrain from cursing out the entire world once every five years. But putting on makeup on top of all that was a bit much.

He came at seven in the morning, as they'd agreed. He offered an uneasy greeting, surveying the hallway like it was a trap; she greeted him with a laugh, though, and even gave him a careless kiss somewhere on his beard. After that, he finally realized that nobody would be fighting with him today. Well, at least not until later. He sat down, agreed to have a cup of coffee a little too energetically when she offered, and instantly regretted it—he thought of his heart, the doctors, the pills he counted out every morning like a beggar with his pennies, meticulous and exacting.

She bustled around the kitchen, as if to show that she wasn't afraid to approach him, wasn't afraid to come face to face with him. She wanted to demonstrate that she wasn't at all afraid, that fear had remained in the past, somewhere back there—five years ago, in a different life, when everything broke and something completely new began, something not particularly pleasant, yet inevitable. So she bustled around, dishes clattering, suddenly fell silent, and gave him a meaningful look—it's still so early, you get it, let's keep it down. He adjusted his glasses and concurred—yeah, let's keep it down, of course, it's still early, just past seven.

He noticed that she still dyed her hair. He also noticed that he didn't really care all that much. In general, he didn't really understand how candid he could be, how to conduct himself, cordially or sincerely. He occasionally glanced at the slow, viscous movement of the minute hand. "I'll wait till nine," he thought. "And then I'll get going. Not a minute longer."

"How are you doing?" he asked eventually.

"Not so hot," she answered honestly. "I'm tired."

"Me too."

"This year has worn everyone out," she added.

"I know."

"When it all started, uh, I mean, last winter, I just didn't know what to do."

"I knew right away. From day one. It was all so simple."

He waited. She didn't ask him to elaborate. He began talking. About staying in his apartment building during the first few days, about everyone leaving or taking shelter down in the metro. About them leaving him their keys: to water their plants, to feed their cats. About those damn cats being afraid of him, hiding from him in wardrobes and under couches—terrified, hungry, standoffish. He told her about sitting through a shelling with the cats, hiding in hallways, hearing their voices—hysterical, piercing. About how he'd shouted to them in the dark, trying to calm them down, but he was frightened by the sound of his own voice.

He also told her about the dog, a German shepherd, that the young couple who lived next door had left behind. They said they were afraid he wouldn't make it, that he'd die before they got where they were going. What's more, they planned to leave by train—it's not like they could take him along. "He's quiet," they said. "Old and quiet. Has no bite—or teeth, for that matter."

"So I come by one morning to take him out for a walk. And I can't figure out what's up with him. He's sitting in the middle of the kitchen, looking at me, but I realize that he can't see me, that he's looking at something only he can see. I'm frightened, I call his owners and ask, 'What's wrong with him?' 'He's blind,' they tell me. 'He was so scared he went blind. When it all started, he went blind. He's kind, though,' they tell me. 'He just can't see you, can't see what you look like.'

"One evening, I take him outside for a walk, in the dark. And a shell lands nearby. The dog bolts, races between some trees, through an arch, and out into the street. And I race after him. And call his name. I can hear him breathing somewhere. But he doesn't see me or come over. And I don't see him either. Can't see him—not even with these damn glasses. And the two of us stand there in the dark, two blind mice, listening to each other's breathing. And we can't find each other."

She nodded inattentively, unable to focus on what he was saying. It all seemed so simple—those first days, a year ago, panic that seeped into your lungs, made you short of breath, the blackness obscuring everything. She remembered those weeks very well, remembered fear being displaced by apathy and despair by irony. Thing is, she didn't want to think about that. And she didn't want to talk about that, not at all. She looked at him and saw that he was glancing desperately at the hand on his watch, like the winning team running out the clock. She looked at him and thought of who they had been ten years ago, of how they tried to break each other, of how easily they fought and then blithely forgave each other. She thought of what had filled their lives back in those days. What was it exactly? Their kitchen, the one they were sitting in now, faced east. It was always sunny in the morning—she remembered that well. There was plenty of sun. In the winter, it shone straight over the roofs; come summertime, it got tangled in the trees, trying to escape like a bird from a cage. Thing is, those trees still stood there out the window; they had aged, yet they were just as tall and dense with branches. No, they hadn't disappeared—there they stood. The sun was gone, though.

She peered out the window, just to double-check. It was gone. The dusty June street, the building opposite them whose windows had been patched up with particle board since last year when the city came under particularly heavy shelling. Streetcar tracks overrun by grass, everything behind the generous greenery comes clearly into view, everything remains close, visible, yet something is lacking, missing; a kind of emptiness emerges beyond all this, a certain disconnect, an incongruity. Like he was speaking about things that didn't truly exist. He spoke with conviction, but it didn't make any of those things more real.

He noticed that she wasn't listening to him; she was looking out the window. He fell silent, tensed up. She turned toward him. Eight-thirty. Time moved as slowly as an old person coming home from the pharmacy.

"When do you have to get going?"

"At nine."

"Can't you stay any longer?"

"I gotta get to work."

"He came back at midnight and didn't get to bed till late. They'll be coming by for him in a few hours, to pick him up."

"I see."

"I wanted you two to spend some time together."

"Yeah."

"How long has it been?"

"Uh, haven't seen him since last winter. We bumped into each other back then, during the first few days. Not for long, though—I was running off somewhere. And he was, too . . ."

"He was going off to fight."

"Okay, don't start."

"All right, sorry. He asked you to come here."

"And here I am."

"He asked me to wake him up once you got here. He said he'd catch up on sleep in the car."

"How is he? Has he changed?"

"Yeah, he's all grown up now. He went straight to his room once he got back. He just sat there, didn't even turn on the light. Maybe he was afraid that something had changed. But everything there is just like it used to be. You remember his room, don't you?"

"Yeah."

"He's really tired."

"I can see that. When's he coming back again?"

"Who knows. Good thing he was able to make it back now."

He didn't know what to say. She did, but she didn't want to get into an argument.

"So," she asked, "should I wake him up?"

He looked at his watch again, tried to picture how much time he had been thinking about all this, rejecting it, refusing to accept it. He thought of them separating, five years ago. He thought of how mad he was at her and then how he got into an accident on the highway. It was like she was the one who'd forced him to speed. He thought of how mad he was at the kid. He tried to picture how much longer he could take this.

"Let him sleep. I'll wait. When's he going to have a chance to sleep in at the barracks? Can you put the kettle on?"

And There's Not Enough Sun to Illuminate Everything

They hadn't seen each other for a while; that's why he didn't recognize her. He considered her as she walked along the row of trees in the park without realizing that she was headed toward him. She approached him, stood opposite the sun. He tried to catch a glimpse of her, but the sun's rays punched him right in the eyes, so he squinted and turned away.

"Hi," she said.

"Hi," he replied. She offered her hand, he shook it, and at that point he recognized her, finally.

She grabbed a chair, took a seat opposite him. The sun kept hitting him in the eyes; she made to sit somewhere else, but he stopped her. "Why can't she just sit still?" he thought. She took him by the hand again, with a gentle, friendly touch. He noticed she didn't have a wedding ring on her finger. "Okay," he thought. "So what?" Twenty-five years of age, she was vivacious, nimble, and talkative. That made things easier—not replying was an option. Dress, sneakers, bouquet of flowers. Apparently, the flowers were for him. She'd brought them but was too embarrassed to hand them to him. "What do I need flowers for?" he thought, offended. He gave her an offended look—those damn sneakers of hers, that story about a streetcar that went the wrong way and made her retrace her steps. By the age of twenty-five, he had learned to take offense and listen, so that is just what he did—took offense and listened.

"Did you even recognize me?" she asked.

"Uh, not at first, no."

"Have I changed?"

"Well, we've all changed. You can see that."

"Yeah."

"The flowers are for me, huh?"

"Yeah." She grew flustered, then broke into laughter and handed him the bouquet brusquely.

"Thanks," he said. "They're pretty. How'd you find me?"

"The old gang said you were in town. I wanted to see you. While I have the chance, you know?"

"Why would you say something like that?"

"Sorry."

There she sat, smiling. He eyed the bouquet. The flowers were somewhat formal looking. The kind people bring to funerals.

"When my grandpa died . . . Do you remember him?"

"No."

"Nobody remembers my grandpa. So nobody believes I had one. Well, he died. Uh, I was still young at the time. And our neighbor, Tolia, came to the cemetery with daisies. He got beat up real bad—so he'd stop it with the flowers. He was making a mockery of the man's life."

"You don't like the flowers, do you?"

"Nah, they're fine. I'll put them in some water a little later."

"I just didn't know what you'd like, what to bring you."

"Well, thank god they're not daisies."

"I haven't seen you in ages."

"How's the old gang?"

"Let her talk," he thought, leaning back. He glanced cursorily at his surroundings and listened.

The trees were tall, their crowns made some noise somewhere up there, high in the air, something was happening above them, something crucial was transpiring, something that compelled them to rustle and sway unhurriedly in the wind. There was plenty of sun, perhaps for the first time in the past few days. After all the rain and clouds, it had finally flopped onto the moving greenery, fully penetrating it, blinding and igniting, making everything blaze and bubble. He would have liked to listen to the trees. Instead, he had to listen to her.

"What should I tell him?" she thought. "What might he be interested in? What had they last spoken about?" And she began telling him about their teachers. Their geography teacher had left with her family. Back in March, after it all started. She got her mom out, too. Then her mom ran away, came back home. Everyone brought her food. The principal had moved in with her relatives, went to their village. She didn't work anymore. After the school got hit, she no longer wanted to educate anyone—she just sat at home. She told him about her mom—she'd taught Ukrainian, and nobody in their class had liked her. She said that her mom had stayed, didn't want to go anywhere. Now she and her mom lived together, which had led to a turf war. They argued a lot, yet they stuck together. Her mom feared most of all that she would get married and leave her all alone. They would fight, then cry and hug it out. Her mom had continued working, but doing it online—what kind of teaching was that? It was kind of demeaning for her.

"What's left of the school?" he asked.

"The frame. It's charred. There's nothing left inside."

"Are they going to rebuild it?"

"What's the point? Everything's online now anyway."

"Are you in touch with anyone from the old gang?" He was finally focused, listening now.

"Yeah. But hardly any of them are still in town. Some of them left, some of them are fighting. Some of them are hiding."

"Hiding from what?" he asked, confused.

"From the war."

"And where are they hiding from the war?"

"At home," she said with a laugh.

"Yeah, like there's no war at home."

"She's pretty," he thought. If he saw her on the street, he'd definitely try to get her number. She was glowing, really. And she'd changed a lot. Nobody'd noticed her in school. Well, it seemed like she hadn't noticed anyone either. A teacher's daughter, no father in the picture, her mom couldn't stand men, she watched her daughter like she was a prison guard. So nobody touched her. And she didn't touch anyone. And she didn't go on dates. Never. Almost never, that is. And she didn't talk to anyone. He tried to remember her voice but couldn't.

"How about you?" she asked. "Are you in touch with anyone from the old gang?"

"Nah. I don't want to see anyone."

"I get it. Want me to go?"

"Oh, no, not at all. Sorry, that's not what I meant. It's good you're here."

"You liked me, admit it," she said with a laugh.

"Everyone liked you," he said indulgently.

"But you told me you had a crush on me. Remember?"

"Now you're making things up."

"Do you really not remember?"

"No."

"Seriously?"

"Thing is, I don't remember anything at all," he said. "A person's memory is like darkness. And you don't know how to illuminate all that. I try to remember what things were like, what we all did, what made us happy. And I just can't. You know, it's like being in the light and then stepping out into the night and trying to make something out. And there's nothing there. Know what I mean?"

"No."

The sun shifted, fell onto his face. He squinted again, yet shied away from slipping into the shade. He faced the sun, feeling it warm him up, ignite him inside, roasting and suffusing everything.

"I should probably get going."

"All right."

"See you around?"

"Yeah, okay." He peeled his eyes open. "Just call me."

"Well, let me have your number."

He said his number aloud. She dialed. His phone rang in his pocket. He didn't bother taking it out.

She'd said her piece. There she sat, silent, fully aware that she ought to get going, that it would be best to let him be by himself, that none of this had any real meaning—her stories, the flowers, the telephone calls. What did have meaning, though? The darkness within him. The darkness she couldn't see, yet felt. She felt it, viscerally. It had meaning. It moved through him, it spoke through him.

She was also thinking of how, as a kid, she used to worry about her mom when everyone would gripe about her, get mad at her, and get all bent out of shape. She never spoke up, but she was worried in her mind; she'd lock up, waiting for all of it to be over, for everyone to start talking about something else. It's a strange feeling when nobody likes your mom, a strict Ukrainian language teacher, principled almost to the point of being rigid. It's truly disheartening. Disheartening and poignant. Brash, smug, condescending—they were overflowing with laughter and grievances. They shouted, rejoiced, goofed around. They loved each other and loved the world around them. Yet they didn't love her mom. So she loved her for everyone. Hopelessly and desperately. Or something like that.

"We all really love you," she said, "and we're proud of you."

"Don't start."

"For real. You're our hero."

"Uh-huh, sure." He finally enjoyed a laugh.

"Hey." She wasn't saying anything, yet she was still there. Eventually, he couldn't take it anymore. "Can I ask you to do something?"

"Sure."

"Keep the flowers."

"How come? Something wrong with them?"

"Nah, that's not it. Uh, what am I supposed to do with them . . . ?"

"You'll put them in some water."

"Keep 'em. You'll walk home holding flowers. Looks pretty."

"All right," she agreed after a moment's thought.

"Don't take offense, though."

"All right."

She took the flowers back, pressed them against her chest, rose from her seat, and stood there for a moment. She held out her hand to him, then left. She walked with a lightness and a certain melancholy, like a woman whose heart had been broken, but who'd been expecting it. At one point, she turned around and waved at him. He waved in reply. She passed through the gate, turned right, disappeared. He took out his phone, found the missed call from her, and added her number.

"Nadia Classmate," he wrote. He tucked his phone away and sat there, waiting for the nurse to come and wheel him back to his ward.

I'll Turn the Lights Out

We were the last ones out—everyone else had left. Misha was supposed to take care of us, and he was supposed to go with us, so he asked us to wait for him. He told us he'd turn off all the lights and lock up the church.

"And count up all the money in the register," Armen laughed, tossing his camera from one hand to the other.

"Don't anger God, pal," Misha laughed in reply.

We went out front, stepped aside, waited. A warm afternoon in early spring, Sunday, the neighborhood by the factory. Empty streets, boisterous birds. The sizable city went about its business; it had unfurled grass on the hills like sheets washed in a river—to dry them, to warm them up—and now it was pausing for a moment in the sun. We looked around, waited, tried not to talk about anything upsetting. Naturally, the best thing to do was to not talk at all. So we didn't.

Misha came out about five minutes later. On the shorter side, slightly unkempt, thin-framed glasses. Old long leather jacket. Looked like a taxi driver who wasn't fond of his job. He locked the church door and yanked the handle to double-check. He did so as though he was closing a garage door on an old car he'd had his whole life. He stood by the entrance, shielded his face from the blinding sun, and looked at us with a hint of irony, like we were a bunch of criminals he'd caught in the act.

"You remember to turn off the iron?" Armen yelled.

"You'll burn in hell," Misha replied without malice, approached us, took out his cigarettes, glanced back at the church, let out a whispered curse, then tucked the pack away again. "How about we get going?" he asked with a nod.

We crossed the churchyard, passed through the gate, and stopped by the car, and Misha finally lit up. We paused for a moment in the sun. Misha in his leather jacket with his red frigid fingers fumbling to clasp a cigarette, Armen in his peacoat, high boots, looking like he was heading to the beach on a cold day, equipped with an unwieldy camera, and the driver—Zhora, I think—whom we'd just met that morning and who looked at us mistrustfully. I, too, wore a jacket; I'd been sporting it since that winter, pretending I wasn't cold. We all pretended that we weren't cold, weren't scared, weren't lonely, that the immediate, excessive presence of death didn't distress us all that much. Several weeks ago, life snapped, time snapped, the sensation of breathing, its cadence and sequence, changed. Now we stood under the vast, bright sky—clustering together, watching each other's backs, waiting for something, listening for something. Hiding fear behind our businesslike manner and panic behind concentration.

The church was cold and large, like a station on a railroad line that led to a dead end—many people had never been here before, and those who had were frankly few in number, so the building was never heated all that well. The main entrance had been refurbished, a recently tiled walkway wound from the gate. Scaffolding stretched along the side wall.

"How long have they been restoring it?" Armen pointed his camera at the church's cupola.

"For as long as I can remember," I replied inattentively.

"It's like a medieval cathedral," Armen said, laughing. "While they're finishing the right wall, the left one collapses."

"Well, it's building something that brings a community together, not having a church at the end," I objected.

The sun fueled a feeling of protection, like you'd stepped into a circle drawn by someone and had become invisible to death. That's why all we wanted to do was stand and wait while a ray of sunlight blinded us, while birds squawked in the sky, while Misha finished his cigarette. It's like when you're a child—you stand next to adults, and they block out the world for you, which makes you feel calm and cozy. You know that if need be they'll protect you, stand up for you. The only thing is that now we're the adults. And the only thing that fills us up is our vulnerability: pervasive, painful, bottomless. And we want to cling to anything that provides us with a feeling of shelter, a feeling of equilibrium. To this damn spring sun, to this Sunday, to this empty city riddled with bullets like a ream of paper. A bunch of freezing forty-year-olds trying to find a place for themselves in a world they've outgrown like a pair of children's shoes. Yet over there, around the corner, the war was going on: death walked the streets, grazing chance passersby, and we hid from it like we were playing hide-and-seek with our high school teacher. This was a strange feeling. A strange and demeaning one. We piled into the van and got going.

Atop an incline, the walls of the university shone brightly

beyond the bridge. Gentle greenery graced the hills, and the ease of this transition, the inaudible warmth which slowly suffused the area, gave everything an air of sorrow and alarm. There was this yearning for different air, different memories—ones unburdened by the smoke of scorched windows and burnt metal, memories without deafening black silence, memories without shattered glass crunching under winter boots. Those were the only memories we had, though. And we didn't have anyone else to keep us company—just the driver, whose silence seemed ostentatious; Armen, whose fashionable peacoat seemed out of place here; and me, so I tried to get Misha talking, which was just what he had been waiting for, actually.

"Misha," I began, "so you're a chaplain, right?"

"Let's not start this," he said, grimacing.

"A man of the cloth. A clergyman."

"There's no need to be envious."

"Yeah, okay. C'mon, tell me."

"Tell you what?"

"What do you tell people about God? Do you have a script or something?"

"Knock it off. The Bible is my script."

"All right. Let's try a different tack. How do you talk about depression?"

"I don't."

"Why not?"

"Depression is a luxury only atheists enjoy. Can I smoke in here?" he asked the driver.

The driver shook his head. Misha grimaced, yet acquiesced. We rode in silence for a bit. Eventually, he couldn't take it anymore.

"I've got a story for you," he began. "A guy volunteered to fight. Didn't tell his mom, though. And he was afraid to. He came to see me like he was going to confession. He was like 'Why don't you give her a call, Father? She'll listen to you.'"

"Father," I said with a chuckle. Misha chuckled in reply.

"I called her. We spoke. At first, she got mad, then she cried, then she started calling."

"Him?"

"Me. I felt like a counselor at Young Pioneers camp."

"Did you quote Scripture?"

"No. She did most of the talking. About her garden, about preserving food. I listened."

"Preserving food?"

"Yep. She didn't call him, she was afraid she'd start yelling. And he didn't call her either, he was too afraid. Well, that's what I'm needed for—to talk to those who are afraid. Depression doesn't have anything to do with that, does it?"

"It doesn't."

"That has to do with love."

"Yeah."

Misha went silent, looked out the window, and turned toward me.

"I helped him get a job. When he got back."

"Doing what? Preserving food?"

"No. At an office. He lost his eyesight. He's blind now. Get it?"

We rode through the city center, zipping through traffic lights that weren't working. The city was as quiet as a soccer field in the winter. Sparse passersby at intersections, windows boarded shut, cats sprawling on rocks. Sunny, spacious, untidy. Like a seaside town right before the start of the season. When we turned past some streetcar tracks and a panorama of a sleepy residential area and the outskirts opened up down below, we spotted, over there on the horizon to the north, two long black strands of smoke. Two cattails. Whatman paper doused with black paint. We parked by a long brick wall. Misha promptly produced his pack of cigarettes; we, too, were in no rush to keep going—it would have been best to return to the city center, hunker down in a bar somewhere, and chat about money and soccer. The thing was that none of the bars were open, the soccer season was over, and money didn't matter much anymore in our town. So Misha finished his cigarette, and we headed out.

We walked through a gate and headed down a path between two rows of trees. The wind had grown stronger, the sun had gone into hiding, and there was this general unease, the way it gets only in wintertime. We hurried, hunching over and tucking our heads into our shoulders so we wouldn't be so cold.

"Do you know the way?" I asked Misha.

"Yeah."

"Have you been here?"

"Twice this month."

We turned down a side path. Up ahead, behind a patch of trees, we saw our crew. We headed toward their silence.

Wind whipped through the cemetery, the trees trembled slightly, flags flapped in people's hands, causing motion and chaos. The crowd didn't fit on the path—friends and loved ones stood by the pit, some folks fanned out around the nearby graves, standing behind the dead slabs of headstones. Almost everyone who had been at the church. We were the last ones there, so we stood off to the side. Priests crowded around the coffin, as did soldiers with flags—they flattened the fresh, red-tinted clay and glanced at the deceased.

"Are you going to say anything?" I asked Misha.

"Let the elders speak." He nodded at the priests.

"Did you know him?"

"No. What about you?"

"I did. And I know his wife."

"Did you talk to her?"

"I did. Back at the church."

"That's good," Misha said. "Talking is the right thing to do. She's hurting now."

"I think she's not the only one."

Misha didn't say anything. I looked at Dina, who stood by the coffin, now frigid and fatigued. Overcoat, dark glasses, heeled boots sinking into the clay, hair fluttering in the wind. She ought to stand there to the very end, ought to see him off. Everyone in the crowd was pretty cold; this Sunday had wound up being too long; walking along the cusp of death, peering into its eyes, was draining, and the blustery weather beat the last remnants of patience out of everyone's bodies. Yet everyone stood there and dealt with it.

The priest sang, words were said, and the coffin was gradually lowered. Misha turned around, trudged down the path between the trees. Armen had squeezed through the crowd and gotten to work. He photographed faces, flags, and clouds. I turned around and followed Misha, eventually catching up to him. We turned to head deeper into the cemetery. We walked, stopped at particularly interesting gravestones, read the names, checked the dates.

"You know what I'm thinking about?" Misha asked.

"What?"

"About how we interpret what makes a death just in completely different ways."

"Is there such a thing as a just death?"

"Of course there is. Everyone is born, everyone dies."

"Christ was resurrected."

"At the cemetery, you get this very particular feeling that you won't be, though. Thing is, you look at the grave of a child who died when they were five, and you can't help but think about the injustice of it. Then you see I. I. Zlodushnyi," he continued, spotting a grave bearing an unusual last name that meant "malicious soul," "born in 1923, who, thank God, lived seventy-seven years, no problem, no questions asked, despite being named that. Am I right?"

"Sure are."

"Well, what questions could we have for the Lord?"

"Yeah . . ."

We turned around, headed back. Our crew was making its way out of the cemetery in little groups, heading back to the cars. Dina stood by the gate at the entrance. She was talking on the phone and thanking someone, flatly. She spotted us, recognized me, and gave a little nod. I nodded in response. Misha placed his hand on his heart.

Armen was waiting by the van. We walked over, and Misha took out his cigarettes.

"Hey," I began, unable to contain myself, "so you're a man of the cloth. You have to be able to explain all of this somehow. This has nothing whatsoever to do with food preservation."

"Sure doesn't."

"And this isn't about depression."

"Nope."

"Then what's up with God?"

"With God?"

"Uh-huh. What's wrong with him?"

"God is love. But there's one place inside him where there is no love."

"What's that supposed to mean? That's not fair."

"Perhaps."

"So his love is not absolute?"

"It is. But there's one place where there is no love."

"Do you know where that place is?"

"No."

Another Month Goes By

Even the dog smelled of strangers. Her mom said that she'd given him a bath just the day before, that he was displeased, had tried to run away, and wound up breaking something. "Watch your step in the bathroom, look out for glass," her mom warned.

She did watch her step, and not just in the bathroom. She'd gotten used to constantly looking down at her feet to keep them in one piece. Especially when she was walking home from the metro. It was irritating—she was well aware that nothing posed a threat here, that she didn't have to be afraid, but she still was; she constantly caught herself thinking as she passed through the park to her apartment complex that she was trying not to veer off the path her neighbors had packed down over the years. There actually were many little shards in the bathroom, though, and it smelled of shampoo. Well, what else was it supposed to smell like?

The dog had grown unaccustomed to her over the past few months. He didn't want to be held; he jumped on the couch and hid behind the cushions. "What are you hiding for?" she thought, without getting angry. "I can smell where you are." Odd scent, odd dog, odd mom. Nothing elicited any emotions. It was like finishing a movie you weren't enjoying.

The only thing that elicited emotion was the shards stabbing her feet. That would hurt; she would feel sorry for herself and would want to cry. She restrained herself, though, and didn't cry—didn't want anyone's sympathy. She sat in the kitchen on the couch, beside the bathed and pleasant-smelling pooch who plainly pissed her off, binged a series, and answered her mom's questions. Her mom tried to be tactful. This was unbearable. Asking questions she didn't even want answers to, telling jokes that weren't funny, constantly suggesting she rest or lie down. She locked herself in the bathroom, turned the water on, sat in a chair, and picked the shards off the floor. Whenever her mom shouted something from the other side of the door, she answered: distinctly, evenly, unemotionally. Two days until the end of her leave. She suddenly realized that she was counting them down.

She woke up earlier than she'd planned. She'd attempted to put herself in the right frame of mind the night before—it's your last day at home, no need to rush to get anywhere, you don't have any errands to run, go ahead and sleep in. You didn't answer any calls, didn't text any friends, didn't agree to meet with anyone. Good work; you made sure you'd be free all day. You may be in a bad mood, the dog, your dog, which you got from a shelter and took care of like he was your own child, gave him all those meds and everything, may be hiding from you and may reek of chemicals, your mom may be bugging you with stories about neighbors who've died, the same neighbors you've both hated your entire lives, but still—you don't have to get up early, you can stay in bed for as long as you want. You don't have a husband, you don't have kids, you don't have a job. Thinking about kids was unpleasant. She thought about them anyway, slept poorly, and woke up early. Her mom was in the kitchen, cooking something delicious and superfluous which nobody would ever eat and trying not to wake her up, so she clattered dishes in a deliberately cautious way.

She lay in bed a long time pretending she was asleep so her mom wouldn't hear her and wouldn't start calling her to the table. Her mom plaintively pretended she didn't hear anything, cooking, washing, clearing the table, changing her clothes, picking up her purse, and going to work, unable to wait any longer, yet opening the bedroom door slightly on her way out, freezing at the threshold, holding her breath, and listening intently to the silence. She'd foreseen this trap, so she, too, held her breath and froze. Her mom let out a sigh of disappointment, shut the door, and shuffled down the stairs. Only then did she crawl out from under the covers. Her lacerated feet probed the floor, warmed by the summer sun. She turned her back toward the slanting rays breaking through the thin old curtains. Early morning, long day. She got up and plodded over to the bathroom in what she'd worn to bed. She brushed her teeth thoroughly, yet reluctantly, fiercely combed her freshly dyed hair, which had suddenly gotten much longer. It suited her, made her look younger and less serious. "Exactly. Can't be taken seriously," she thought, irritated, and was about to step out of the bathroom, but then she glanced at herself one more time and thought that she actually liked herself: tall, dazzling, discontented. She thought that she didn't find herself irritating, that not even her scar irritated her—a cute scar stretching above her collarbone, like a little drawing, attracting attention, you wanted to touch it, you wanted to touch her skin, warm and gleaming. She thought that she hadn't felt this way for a long time. It was as though somebody had turned on the lights and everything had suddenly become visible, easily understood, to her utter surprise—how come she hadn't seen that earlier? "Yeah, how did I not see that?" she thought, irritated, turned off the lights, and walked toward the kitchen.

The dog awaited her at the table. As soon as she entered, he made a big show of turning around and hiding under the cushions.

"You little rascal," she thought, and tried figuring out what her mom had concocted in the kitchen that morning. Her mom cooked plentiful and chaotic meals. So she sat there, chewing on something, tasting how delicious it was, and chastising herself—I eat too much, don't take care of myself, I'll be grossed out by myself if I balloon up.

"I'm already grossed out," she thought. Lethargic, hot, and delicious. She felt like sitting in the kitchen, continuing to chow down on her mom's breakfast, and being mad at the whole world.

She also thought that it would be nice to come up with something that would take all day, something to do. Maybe she should call someone, meet up with someone, or go to the store, at the very least. But then she pictured the sun-soaked street, pictured herself standing in the middle of all that sun—tall, conspicuous, wearing something that wasn't really her thing, civilian clothes—something bright and beautiful, that is. She decided not to go anywhere, to sit at home, binge a series, and wait for a text.

On Monday, everyone texted, naturally. They texted about anything and everything. About the car that had to be picked up from the shop, about the Kid, who tried skipping treatment, just ran out of the ward. She had to call him, but he wasn't picking up, and she called their unit, shouted, argued, got the Kid's relatives' phone numbers, threatened someone, then apologized, then, aggrieved, didn't answer any calls for a long time, then called them back and explained something or other, and when it already seemed as though everything had come together—with the car and the Kid—she put her phone aside and suddenly burst into tears. She felt sorry for herself, then she thought that she felt sorry for her mom, too—by herself for weeks on end, no visitors, no help—and that dog, she felt sorry for him in her own way, too. A good yet wicked beast. She felt sorry for everyone, and there was this nagging feeling that everyone felt sorry for her, too, that everyone had been treating her like she was helpless and defenseless, that nobody took her seriously anymore, especially the women who called her all day, always demanding something from her. Yes, especially those women. After she'd had a good cry and calmed down, her mom came back from work.

She said that she'd seen their neighbor. He'd disappeared at the beginning of it all, in March. Nobody knew where he was and what had become of him, while she, her mom, that is, suspected that he'd gone over to the other side, that he wouldn't be coming back.

"So," her mom said, "he showed back up, said that he'd been sitting it out at his brother's in a village on the other side of the Dnipro. But he couldn't take it anymore, so he came back. He said he'd been to the pharmacy to pick up some meds. You know, he showed me those pills with such tenderness, like they were something good, those pills of his, like they were something to be happy about. And I took one look at those pills and I couldn't fathom how he was still alive—he's sick to the core. You see?"

"Yeah."

"Do you take any meds?" her mom asked severely.

"No," she answered. "I used to. To calm my nerves."

"What about now?"

"I don't take anything now."

"How come?"

"I've calmed down."

Her mom shook her head in an affectedly bitter way—yeah, yeah, not fooling me—yet didn't say anything and then began cooking again, commenting on the Turkish TV series they were watching from time to time and rebuffing the dog, who'd woken up and grown incongruously active that evening, with her foot.

She listened to her mom, watched TV listlessly, and when the plot had these Turkish folks divvying up some esteemed deceased relative's inheritance and brother turned against brother as they were dividing up this wealth that had been earned honestly, she couldn't take it anymore.

"I was wondering," she said, "why didn't you and dad want any more children?"

Her mom put the pan aside, looked at her, thought of making a funny quip but then reconsidered.

"Because with your dad," she said, "about the only thing I wanted to do was hang myself."

"Don't get angry now."

"I'm not."

"Didn't he love children?"

"Everyone loves children," her mom replied. "It's just that not everyone wants to take care of them. I mean you can't even take care of your own dog, you dumped him on me."

"All right, all right," she said, growing anxious.

"Am I wrong about anything?" Her mom turned toward the stove and calmed down. "More children, you say."

She snapped, stood up ostentatiously, grabbed her cup of tea, and went to her room. She wanted to slam the door, but she thought that then she'd have to start a fight, make up, and calm herself down, so she just shut it gingerly and crawled under the covers: in her clothes, with her tea, miserable, agitated.

She lay there and looked at something in front of her. She'd tossed her phone aside, occasionally glancing at it desperately—who will text me, who else will text me, who will text right now?

An unknown number flashed. Typically, she didn't answer calls from unknown numbers. Don't answer, she told herself, then answered.

The voice was female, fatigued, disgruntled. The kind of voice typically used to talk about problems. She, too, constantly spoke in a voice like that.

"Are you the one who knows something about our little Andriusha?" she was asked.

"About Andriusha?" Before, she would have gotten angry, but now she was wondering what was going on with Andriusha.

"I was told that you spoke to the doctor."

"About what?"

"About Andriusha."

"And what about him?"

"He doesn't want to undergo treatment."

"How did this happen?" she thought. How did it happen that she had been lying around for the past three days, wrapped up in a blanket, lying around and suffering, mad at the whole world, like the whole world wanted to cause her problems. And what problems does she have? She has a mom, a dog—a freshly bathed dog, at that—they love her. She has a home, her own room. Everyone needs her, she takes care of all kinds of things, the world would stop and stand still without her, people call her, but "the people calling," she thought, growing anxious, "aren't the ones who should be, and the ones who should don't call! And who is this Andriusha guy? Andriusha, Andriusha . . ." She still couldn't figure that out.

"Hey," she said, interrupting the fatigued voice that kept talking about Andriusha, "who are you?"

"Me?" The voice was flustered. "I'm his sister."

"You're probably talking about the Kid, aren't you?"

"What kid?"

"The one who doesn't want to undergo treatment. He's your little brother, right?"

"Right."

"That's him, then."

"We call him Andriusha."

"Does he like that nickname?"

"Dunno," the voice admitted wearily.

"All right. I'll give him a call, I'll talk to him. He will undergo treatment."

"Thank you," the voice said. "I'll send you the card number."

"Card?"

"Bank card."

"Andruisha's? Dammit, the Kid's?"

"No, mine."

"What do I need your card for?"

"Well, you know . . ." The voice was flustered.

"Okay," she said. "Goodbye. Don't call me anymore."

"What the hell?" she thought. Maybe I should adopt her while I'm at it? Gotta call the Kid and knock some sense into him. He's got everyone on high alert. Have to tidy up around here, this place looks like an animal's burrow or something. And it's time to get going already. There's nothing to do here. There's no one here, nothing's keeping me, tomorrow morning I'll toss my things in my backpack and get going. I'm falling apart, don't feel like myself—I just hid under the covers, closed my eyes, and thought that another summer was going by, and in the summer, everything seems so vast, so unreal, and you realize that everything is so real, so close, and you can forget about everything—just close your eyes and forget—and all this can just disappear, and this long, endless, exhausting spring, the one when everything has changed, and this evening when I didn't wind up getting the call I was expecting, even though it's so easy—just pick up the phone and call, what's so hard about that? Everything can disappear if she just closes her eyes, lies in the darkness, and doesn't think about these few months, about those few meetings, about strangers' homes, about cold hotel rooms, about harshness and trust, about an attempt to tie impossible and painful things together, about that one time she had unprotected sex, and this general feeling of being unprotected, vulnerable, which emerged once he came into her life.

Summer will go on, everything will be like it used to be, everything will fall into place, she'll be with her people, she'll do what she's used to, she'll finally calm down, help the Kid, and pick up the car. And her damn period will finally start tomorrow.

She got up, opened the door so she could hear her mom, turned off the light so her mom wouldn't pester her with any more talking, went back to bed, and began falling asleep. The dog ran over, circled the room, got up on her bed with a businesslike leap, curled up at her feet, and fell asleep, carefree.

And she didn't get her period.

Beasts

The school first got hit in March 2022. Several windows were knocked out, the roof sank. The city was empty, and the school was in a dangerous area, so nobody was in a rush to repair it. The principal sent somebody by; he looked around, took some pictures, and ran for it, taking a couple of plastic chairs with him. The principal was all worked up; she called the Department of Education, they promised to do something, then it started raining and raining, flooding the classrooms. After that, some municipal employees arrived, patched the roof, boarded up the windows.

In May, the Russians pulled back from the city, and flowers and grass overran the schoolyard. It was sunny outside, quiet and scary in the hallways. Nobody had begun repairing the building; classes were being held online, the principal had gone to Prague and wasn't planning on coming back. Nonetheless, she called their oldest teacher, Pal Ivanych, and asked him to come to work from time to time to keep an eye on the place.

Pal Ivanych was single, lived in a house a few blocks from the school, always argued with his neighbors, didn't like his students, and feared the administration. So he immediately agreed. He couldn't work online, since he didn't have internet at home . . . or a computer, for that matter. For a while, two students would come to his house for lessons: under bombardment, between air-raid alerts. But Pal Ivanych would yell at them, so they weren't too eager to study. Moreover, they didn't like being in Pal Ivanych's home. Didn't like his black tea with no sugar in it, didn't like his withered flowers, didn't like the slippers, which once belonged to various women, that they had to wear when they took off their shoes at the door. Didn't even like the piano—it was as cold as a gravestone. So they stopped coming. Pal Ivanych openly admitted that to the principal; she shut her eyes and asked him to look after the school.

Pal Ivanych woke up, poured plain tea in his thermos, boiled two eggs, cut off a neat slice of black bread, tucked it all in his briefcase, and went to the school. He opened the doors, sat in the hallway, and sipped his tea for a long time. Didn't go outside. It was warm, sunny, and pleasant outside. One time, he stuck around until evening, taking out a book and reading until sunset. Then he rose reluctantly, left the book open on a desk, and went home. The following morning, he returned, intending to finish it, but come evening he traipsed home with pages still unread. The following morning, he showed up hauling a mattress on his back. In the evening, he placed the mattress on the floor, lay down, and covered himself with an old women's coat he'd also lugged over from his house. Couldn't fall asleep. Stars shone outside the window. Before the war, he'd never seen a starry sky in the city. It was worrying and alarming. It was quiet and empty. Smelled of a painted floor and the women's coat.

He'd been living at school ever since. In the morning, he'd go home, make breakfast, then return. He roamed the schoolyard, which had been slowly overrun by grass. The grass got taller and taller, encircled the trees in the school garden, thrust through the paving stones. Pal Ivanych took a chair outside, sat down, and looked over the fence at the street. There was some activity, some life going on over there: cars drove by, bikes rolled along, some pedestrians passed. He was left alone, nobody called him, his phone—an old Nokia—lay on a desk in the hallway, idle and losing its charge.

One morning he discovered that his phone was completely dead and could no longer be charged. "Well, all right then," he thought, and went for a walk in the schoolyard. Three days later, some students' parents ran over to the school: the principal couldn't get hold of him, she got all worked up and worried about him, thought that something might have happened to the school, called one of the parents, asked them to go take a look. There wasn't anything to look at—Pal Ivanych was sitting under the awning out front reading an old edition of Castaneda, from the late eighties, which he'd found in the library. The parents chided him and sent him home. He went, yet kept the key. He returned the following morning.

Several days after that, at the beginning of August, it was his birthday. He wasn't planning on celebrating. Yet his students came; they gave him a new phone—an inexpensive one—charged it just in case, and put his old SIM card in it. And then, a few days after that, the school got hit again.

It got hit in the early morning, while he was asleep. He'd had trouble falling asleep; he read, put the book aside, picked it up again, put on his grungy glasses, and set about fishing letters out of the text. He found Castaneda unconvincing, so he returned to crime fiction, reading without sympathizing with anyone and anticipating the resolution. It landed in the schoolyard, behind the building. He was buried under shattered glass, dust caked the floor, the window frames sagged like broken masts. Pal Ivanych took out his phone and made a call, but nobody answered—Prague was an hour behind.

Volunteers arrived in the afternoon. Someone had told them to stop by the school. Pal Ivanych was there, sitting out front and fiddling with his new phone, when a shabby van pulled up to the gate. There were three of them: a young woman of about thirty and two guys, one chubby, the other missing an arm. The young woman was in the driver's seat. And not just in the van. She was slim, tired, and always yelling at everyone. It seemed like her team loved her, but was trying not to show it, which made her yell even more. She wore canvas shoes, cargo pants, and a black T-shirt with a faded print on it. Her arms were all scratched up. Chubby was kind; he chuckled at everything, scrutinized the schoolyard, clearly intrigued, and carried a suitcase full of tools. It looked as though he was the only one capable of working. He wore a dark windbreaker, stretched-out sweatpants, and combat boots. Lefty stood behind everyone, listening to their brigadier yelling and nodding in agreement, just in case. He wore a T-shirt, as if to demonstrate that he was, indeed, missing an arm, shorts, and sneakers—no laces, just Velcro, like he was a schoolboy. They approached Pal Ivanych, greeted him. The brigadier shook hands with him, then folded her arms behind her back. Chubby took a long time to remove his construction gloves so they could shake hands, then just as long to put them back on. Lefty offered a greeting with his left hand—obviously.

“Cats?” Pal Ivanych asked cordially, nodding at her arms.

“Cats,” she replied flatly and went into the school.

“Those are demons clawing their way out of her,” Chubby chuckled. “She’s the one scratching them.”

“Cut the chatter!” the brigadier shouted, already in the hallway by then.

Chubby smiled, yet stopped talking. He followed the brigadier, Lefty in tow. Pal Ivanych thought for a second, then also filed in behind them.

They stopped in the hallway in front of the busted windows. Chubby produced a tape and began taking measurements, then jotted something down in a notebook. The brigadier walked around, took pictures, then called someone and began arguing. Her voice was hoarse; she argued gleefully. Lefty stood off to the side, looking at everything with a certain skepticism.

Pal Ivanych tried striking up a conversation with the brigadier. Tried complaining a little, whining, and bellyaching. The brigadier looked at him, scratched her arm, and continued arguing optimistically with whoever had called her. Eventually, Pal Ivanych started to get the feeling it was him she was arguing with, so he went over to Chubby, since he was the only one of them not being aggressive.

“Why do they target schools?” he asked. “This is an educational institution.”

“Exactly,” Chubby chuckled.

“There aren’t any soldiers here.”

“Sure aren’t.”

“So why do they do it?”

“Well, what do you think?”

Pal Ivanych was frightened, and he refrained from replying. He headed down a long, hollow hallway. Heavy stripes of sun settled on the floor. Shattered glass crunched ceremoniously under his feet.

"Wait up," Lefty suddenly shouted at his back.

Pal Ivanych cringed and stopped.

"Wait up." Lefty walked over briskly and placed his hand on Pal Ivanych's shoulder. "Let's take a look around, make sure everything else is in working order."

"It is," Pal Ivanych assured him.

"Let's take a look around." Lefty pressed down on his shoulder.

So they took a look around. The classrooms were quiet; the air was murky, like they'd been flooded with river water. They went into the auditorium. On the small stage stood two pianos, one alongside the other. Heavy, dark, looking like injured animals.

"They were damaged back in March," Pal Ivanych said, "the first time the school got hit. I kept them covered with blankets all through spring . . . wasn't much, but you know . . ."

"May I?" Lefty walked across the auditorium, went up on stage, lifted the lid of one of the pianos, and began tapping the keys with his index finger. He looked like someone who'd decided to type something out but didn't really know how.

Pal Ivanych suddenly thought that he'd never seen anyone play an instrument like that—with one finger on their only hand. The only hand they had left.

"Gotta repair them," he said.

"Well, we don't repair pianos." Lefty stopped, shut the lid, and got down off the stage.

"Who does?"

"These days? Nobody."

"Nobody in the whole city?" Pal Ivanych asked, bewildered. "There's gotta be somebody."

"Nobody. It's been a while since you were in town, hasn't it?"

"Yeah."

"I can tell. Been sitting here guarding pianos? Everything has changed over there." Lefty waved at someplace out the window. "Go take a look one of these days."

"I don't want to," Pal Ivanych said quietly, stepped out into the hallway, and plodded outside.

Chubby had already measured and recorded everything; he stood on the steps, smoking contentedly and humming something. Pal Ivanych walked over and timidly eyed him from the side.

"I showed your colleague our pianos. They were damaged. Nice pianos. They really are. I asked whether there was anyone in the city who could repair them. 'Nobody,' that's what he said. Nobody? For real?"

"Nobody."

"So now what? These are state assets we're talking about."

"State assets," Chubby said, "your students are state assets. They don't come here, do they?"

"Nah."

"Exactly. Keep 'em at home, they'll be out of harm's way there. Now those are state assets."

"Hey, listen," Pal Ivanych said, growing agitated. "What are you even saying? So let's just burn everything down, wreck everything? Let's use all our tools for kindling, and all the libraries while we're at it. See how that goes."

"All the libraries?" Chubby turned toward him. "How come? What are you reading now?"

“Castaneda,” Pal Ivanych replied, flustered.

“And do you like him?”

“No.”

“Well, there you have it.”

Pal Ivanych fell into an aggrieved silence. Chubby appeared to have worked himself into a frenzy, too; all flushed, he lit another cigarette. Lefty was hiding out in the van, the brigadier stood by the gate, arguing—quietly now, somewhat wearily.

“Still,” Pal Ivanych said, “I don’t agree with you. What did they have to break the pianos for?”

“Pianos?” Chubby asked. “They broke my mom’s spine. With a beam.”

“I hate them,” Pal Ivanych said.

“Who?”

“The people who started all of this.”

“Well, who was that?” Chubby asked suddenly, speaking slowly and quietly.

The trees, tall, cheerful, swayed stridently. Pal Ivanych thought that he’d have to go home to sleep tonight. That gave him an unpleasant feeling. He produced his phone, started looking for something.

“New phone,” he said, “still haven’t really gotten used to it. Got it as a gift.”

“Your students?”

“Yeah.”

“Do they like you?”

“Nah.”

“You like them?”

“I do.”

He stood there, pressing the buttons slowly, with great concentration.

"My previous phone," he said, "was so old. Didn't change a thing after I put everyone's numbers in there about ten years ago. But then I got a new one. All my contacts were saved. Now I've been sitting here all day . . ."

"Doing what?"

"Crossing them out."

"Crossing who out?"

"Everyone who's died since it started. I'm at the letter 'D.'"

Who You're Going to Remember

Their voices are hoarse, like they've all come down with a cold. Or they've just been standing outside on a blustery day. They mill around, shouting over each other. They all know each other, they're all from the same crew, they're all from the same unit. They've clustered together in the middle of a large hall doused in sprawling spring sunlight, trying to act natural. Nevertheless, they occasionally glance at the heavy closed doors, seemingly anticipating some sort of surprise from over there. They stay in a pack like schoolchildren, don't pay attention to anyone else, hide their hands behind their backs, and are afraid of tracking mud—the carpet in the hall is expensive and plain, the kind of carpet given to people you don't need anything from. A smoke would be nice now, but our CO told us to stay put: it's a state-run institution, the people working here are running on enthusiasm, so punctuality is off the table, and it's best just to wait a little.

"This is a family affair," our CO said. "Like a funeral, a christening, that sort of thing. You can't plan ahead. Just sit tight and wait for them to call us in."

We were late—twenty minutes or so. We were buying flowers—took us a long time to choose, to pack them up. We raced through the city, hurrying, showed up late. We thought that there was no point in even going, that everything was already over, but we came anyway. It's not like we were going to turn around and head back. The front doors were locked, so we had to go around; a group of elderly people, drained by their duties, stood by the staff entrance: men in old-fashioned formal jackets, women in motley uncomfortable dresses, waiting their turn, seemingly hoping everyone would just forget about them. We stepped inside, went up a few stairs, then reached a large, well-lit room with national symbols on the walls—more sad than solemn.

"Where should we go?" we asked a woman who was sticking something on a bulletin board. She waved her scissors at an imposing set of doors. We opened them and found ourselves in the hall where everyone was. We, too, started shouting over everyone, offered greetings, self-conscious about our heavy boots, paid no mind to the people we didn't know, and apprehensively eyed the closed doors.

Once we'd greeted everyone, we stepped aside, standing against the wall. A cameraman began fiddling with his gear. I looked out the window. People were coming over to talk. Out the window, it was early spring: sunny, dry, dusty, brimming with restless birds. Cars pulled into the parking lot, forcing flocks to take flight, like dogs dashing after carefree fowl in the spring. Entire families, tensely solemn and boisterous, piled out of the cars. The men squinted at the sun, the women were taking care of things, the children craved to escape all of it, though they couldn't quite get their bearings.

Some doors opened; everyone froze for a split second, then turned around and scrutinized what was behind those doors, what to expect, what to relish. Our CO came in, followed by a woman with a bizarre hairdo. The woman wore a green outfit; she was in charge here, yet she felt less than confident next to him. He sensed that and took advantage of the situation.

"Okay, is everyone here?" he asked. "Is anybody out having a smoke?"

Everyone was there, which pleased our CO immensely. Like that was what mattered, that nobody was out smoking while he was gone, that nobody was smoking without him. I think he was just used to counting heads, to being responsible for everyone.

"Now we're all going to go into the next room, stand along the wall, and listen to Tetiana." He looked back at the woman in green.

"Tetiana Volodymyrivna," she corrected him in a voice that elicited trust despite being unpleasant, indicating that she was to be addressed formally, by name and patronymic.

"Tetiana Volodymyrivna, that is," our CO said. "First the cameraman, next the bride and groom, then the rest of the bunch. Got that? Let's go tie the knot."

Everyone laughed, began jostling, and moved forward.

The groom was first to enter. He walked with confidence, yet it looked as though he was being goaded along. The bride walked behind him, chuckling at everyone. She was slim and on the smallish side, with short, light-brown hair. Her dress fit her well, which is almost never the case for brides. She held a bouquet, fanned herself with it; overall, it was plain to see that she viewed all this with a certain sense of irony and had agreed to it purely out of respect for the groom. The groom sensed that and grew nervous. He was big, conspicuous, wore his military fatigues, and had let someone pin on the medal he typically kept tucked away at home between his athletic trophies. It was the bride who'd wanted him to wear it. "If this is gonna be a circus, let's do it right," she'd said. So he was simultaneously self-conscious about the medal, his large, gasoline-stained hands, and his mom and dad, who were crying as if they felt sorry for him. His parents probed the bride warily and distrustfully, like they hadn't had time to get a good look at her before that. Yet as soon as the cameraman emerged nearby, they automatically began smiling: hopelessly, despairingly, through tears.

Tetiana Volodymyrivna's spiel was brief and garbled. She would have spoken longer, but there was a line out in the hallway. She spoke with a lack of sincerity; something kept her from being sincere—it was either the stodginess she'd acquired at work or the fact that she hadn't fully lost her conscience. Nevertheless, she said a few words about having a new family, about the overall sense of joy being felt, touched upon international affairs, outlined the main domestic issues, matters of social welfare, developing areas outside major cities, education and healthcare reform, matters of culture, sport, and the weather during the summer season, wished the bride and groom happiness, as an afterthought of sorts, and told everyone to congratulate their parents, insinuating that they'd be the ones who'd have to clean up this mess.

Once she'd finished and our CO had kissed her hand, somewhat awkwardly, she disappeared through the doors, leaving us alone with the new family. Our CO lifted his hand with great pleasure; everyone fell silent. The groom's mom couldn't stop, though. She continued crying a little.

"Let's take a smoke break, take some pictures, and head home," our CO said.

Everyone cheerfully careened toward the bride and groom, congratulated them, left them armfuls of obnoxiously bright flowers, and went outside. The cameraman and I waited our turn, congratulated both of them, gave them our flowers, wished them luck, and then headed outside.

We went over to our crew; they were engaged in an animated discussion about what they'd seen.

"Yehor," someone said, referring to the groom, "prepared a lot. He learned a song. About moms. But Natka," he said, referring to the bride, "asked him not to sing it."

"How come?" I asked, confused.

"Well, she said, 'when you marry your mom, then you can sing it.'"

"Makes sense."

"Yeah, makes sense," everyone agreed.

There were a lot of people. The sun warmed the asphalt. It was calm, like two years ago. What was this gang doing two years ago? Making money. Decent, honest, good money that allowed them to lead decent lives and not have any pangs of conscience. They studied, traveled the world, lived their lives. Now they stood here outside this wedding venue on asphalt scarred by shrapnel, happy for their friend who'd married well and thinking their own private thoughts. Their private thoughts remained, by and large, back there, beyond the winter that ended two years ago; here, the only thing that was theirs was this gang, boisterous and unbearable. So all they could do was stick together; there wasn't anything else to cling to here.

"Do you know his parents?" We had been standing outside for some time before we were called back inside for a group photo. I stood next to Sasha, our CO's deputy, who was actually in charge of everything around here. He was tall, dark-haired, and angry. He stood there, smiling and smoking in a juvenile way, not taking any deep drags.

"Yeah. He joined us before this phase of the war, back in 2018. He was just a kid."

"What do they do?"

"They're professors."

"Professors? What do they teach?"

"Nothing. They've been vendors at the market for the past twenty years."

"They don't exactly love her, do they?"

"They love him. They're worried. He's in the military."

"She is too."

"Well, that's not their problem."

"Where are her parents?" I asked. "Couldn't come?"

"Yeah," Sasha replied. "They're in an occupied area."

"Couldn't get out in time?"

"Didn't want to."

"And what are they doing there?"

"Working."

"For who?"

"For their retirement."

Sasha finished smoking and flicked his cigarette butt toward a garbage can.

"She has a brother," he said. "He's younger. He stayed, too. Sent her a picture this morning. Of a severed pig's head. Congratulations of sorts."

He turned around, headed inside. Everyone else followed suit. The civilians milling around by the doors made way for him. The women looked on with despair, the men stayed silent. Two younger guys stood a bit off to the side: tracksuits with something printed on them, new, white sneakers—cheap ones.

"You gettin' married, too?" I asked them.

They tensed up but decided not to start anything with me.

"Here to see our brother get married," the guy closer to me said.

"How old is he?"

"Twenty."

"Why's he getting married so young?"

"Love," the guy said after a moment's thought.

"Your parents don't mind?" I decided to keep the conversation going.

"Mom doesn't mind, Dad's not around."

"Is he off fighting?"

"He's in jail."

"All right, well, I'm gonna get going. I wish the bride and groom good health."

"Okay."

For some reason, everyone formed a long line once again, then came up to the newlyweds and congratulated them one more time. The soldiers who'd known the groom a while came up to his parents and congratulated them, too. His mom hugged everyone; she'd stopped crying and calmed down. His dad, on the other hand, was somewhat confused; he wasn't used to people thanking him, to not being yelled at. The line was endless. Everyone had a lot to say, offered plenty of well-wishes, and hugged the bride cautiously. The sun hit the windows through heavy, dusty curtains. There was this feeling of summer, this feeling of endlessness, when summer has just begun, when there's so much of it that you can't handle it, you drown in it, like it's a river that's been warmed all the way through, feeling it flow past you, go on by you, leave you all alone amid its warm, thick course, amid temporal viscosity, amid the past and the future.

It took the cameraman a while to arrange everyone; our CO walked around and shouted at us, without malice, as we were jostling, getting in each other's way, and changing places. Nonetheless, not everyone could fit in the shot; some people were blocking others and some people couldn't find a spot for themselves. Eventually, our CO couldn't take it anymore.

"All righty now," he said, "let's do this like soccer teams do. Everyone in the front sits, everyone in the back stands. Got that?"

Everyone got it. We all fit in the shot.

Sasha and I sat next to each other, felt like soccer players, and took in the cameraman's commands.

"I'd like to take a look at this picture in twenty years," Sasha said.

"You will," I assured him.

"If I'm alive," he replied. "At home, we have a picture in our family album of my old man during his time in the army. They were sitting like this, somewhere in the woods. My old man used to love looking at it and reminiscing. He remembered everyone."

"Well, you'll remember everyone, too," I said, laughing. "Won't you?"

"Not sure about that," he said with a chuckle. "I don't know half of them as it is."

"Attention!" the cameraman shouted, and everyone fell silent.

The doors opened. The two younger guys came inside. They saw our team and froze.

“Come on in!” our CO shouted encouragingly, without taking his eyes off the camera.

The two younger guys joined their crew; we followed them with our eyes. Their group stood on the other side of the room waiting their turn. They stood quietly, examining the soldiers without making any comments or hollering back and forth. They weren’t even staring at their phones—they were mostly older people who didn’t have smartphones.

The twenty-year-old groom just couldn’t get used to his striped jacket—too wide, too long. He was long-limbed, so skinny, and not too sure of himself. Possibly because of the jacket. The bride had tar-black hair, deep, dark eyes, and scorchingly bright makeup. She held the groom’s hand like someone might hold an umbrella—rather carelessly, so others wouldn’t think that she really needed it, yet also rather carefully, so she wouldn’t forget it. The bride looked at the soldiers without trying to hide her interest and smiled with restraint. The groom, though, tried not to look at the soldiers, averting his eyes and growing anxious. He swept his eyes across everyone and lowered his head. But then he gingerly touched her belly and looked at everyone again. This time, with pride.

Nobody Will Ask for Anything

They said there would be an around-the-clock curfew on Independence Day. Most likely, the city would be shelled. Best to wait it out.

"Got the day off?" Artem asked.

"Yep," Goner replied. "Normal people do, at least. I was asked to deliver a package outside the city. For some kids."

"Those kids can wait another day."

"They come from a broken home or something like that."

"Of course they do."

"I can go by myself."

"You sure can."

They sat in the living room in front of the dead TV and empty table and scrolled through the news. The same news, the same videos, the same statistics, dark and endless. Sometimes they'd come across something funny. They'd read it aloud, nod—yeah, that's funny.

Before the war, Goner had started remodeling. He began in the bedroom: moved furniture out, stripped the wallpaper, brought in the new stuff. And then the war started. His family left; he stayed. The apartment was more or less safe: first floor, old building, not too far from the city center. It hadn't been hit yet, so he occasionally had guests over, and they spent the night. Consequently, they lived simply, weren't finicky; the apartment itself looked like a hostel whose guests hadn't paid for a while. The bedroom was still stripped bare and cluttered, so everyone hung out in the living room. A bunch of sleeping bags covering the large sofa bed, several more on the floor with blankets on top of them, pillows, a table, a TV—the remote had gone missing back in the spring—a bookshelf without any books, pots full of withered flowers. Sometimes it was cozy here, but generally it was just unbearable.

In the late evening, Goner suddenly realized that supper still had to be made.

"You don't have to." Artem tried to stop him. "Who's going to eat it?"

Goner had already gone into the kitchen, though; he clattered jars in the fridge, took out less than fresh groceries, and sawed stale bread. Goner seemed to be fine with this way of living, the kind of living when the trash isn't taken out simply because there isn't any. Everyone had swiftly and painlessly grown accustomed to the new rules: find a place to sleep, don't plan anything in particular, don't commit to too much. You can sleep in a sleeping bag, you can use someone else's shampoo, you can eat whatever. There's as much time as there is air you can breathe. As long as there is something to breathe, there is time. Nothing else seems all that compelling or necessary. Wrecked perceptions about everyday life, the city's altered breathing, the thick air of a tired August—nighttime neared, it was quiet, the people in the building seemed scared of making their presence known. The untouched supper grew cold, and they went through the news again, then went to bed, each in his own sleeping bag. They agreed to sleep in: they had the day off, didn't have much to do, the whole day was wide open.

They woke up at six. They pretended to be asleep for a bit. Eventually, one of them snapped first and reached for his phone. They could get up then. Goner went to put on the kettle. Then they waited and waited for it to cool down. They looked at the hot mugs like they were duties someone had contrived for them. At nine, they couldn't take it anymore and decided to get going. Goner hopped in the driver's seat. Artem sat next to him and surveyed the van: an old blanket, winter boots on the floor, boxes of humanitarian aid. The tall trees gave the morning a certain freshness; the day was primed to be a long one, there weren't any people on the streets, but you could imagine them.

They pulled out into the street, turned left at an intersection, and pulled out into an avenue. There was a piercing emptiness. The traffic lights were out. There was no one around. Artem found himself thinking that he'd never seen the city so empty. He'd had to go somewhere or other countless times after midnight or in the early morning, especially during his college days, when he simply didn't have any money to take a taxi. But even then, he'd always come across frightened, lonely passersby, as well as street cleaners and dog owners. Nevertheless, the warmth exuded by people, their breathing, could be felt. Now, things were just kind of strange, frighteningly so: the city kindled by August, the blinding panorama of the avenue, the sun-scorched skies on the horizon, the park laden with greenery, and beyond all this—not a single voice, not a single movement, as if all the pedestrians, all the city's residents, all the children and adults were hiding behind trees, playing some sort of game only they were privy to, hiding out and concealing something, which caused even more anxiety. After all, they're right around here. But where? It's like you've slipped into a dream, and you're fully aware that it's a dream, that it can't be right, that something is off, something has been disrupted and distorted, that as soon as you peek around the corner, peek behind a tree or storefront, everything will fall back into place, everything will become clear. Also, something else got in the way, enhancing the particularly unreal quality of all this. Artem lowered his window. "What's the matter?" he thought. "What's getting in the way?" Birds, the birds' squawking in the trees—clamorous, tireless. The birds could continue squawking, filling the morning silence and ignoring this emptiness. Someone had forgotten to warn them. They were left in the dark. "The city of birds," Artem thought, and rolled up his window.

They slowed down at a checkpoint. It was quiet, yet there was this general feeling that there was someone there. A young soldier came out, asked for the password, checked their papers, didn't find anything to hassle them about, let them go, and quickly went back behind the cinder blocks.

The sun-soaked square, the blinding, stretched-out central street, the park, the river. They zipped across a bridge, turned down a side alley, and began taking old streets out of the city. The city without any people in it was akin to a case after the instrument had been removed—wide-open and incongruous.

"No one around. This is nice," Goner said.

"There's no such thing as 'no one around,'" Artem objected.

Even the train station was empty. It seemed as though there was no one left in the city except them and the soldiers at the checkpoints.

"Strange . . ." Artem thought. "I've driven down these streets a hundred times during the past six months, taking people out or bringing something in. But I never noticed just how many empty houses there are."

Dark, opaque windows. Typically, you don't pay any attention to that. Typically, the presence of pedestrians brings everything to life. Yet when there's no one on the streets and there's no one to ask for directions, or any other guidance, you instantly realize that nobody lives here or ever will again. And that there's no need to.

They passed through several more checkpoints, stopping, letting their eyes linger, and exchanging several phrases each time. It was a hot morning, summer was coming to a generous end, autumn could be felt beyond the light and slightly bitter air, and you could breathe deeply and abruptly and feel this tinge of cold, of cooling. These are the sweetest and saddest days of equilibrium, when the inevitability of the cold and the regularity of death seem so sharp and so just.

They took the Kyiv highway, turned into a small town, rolled through a railroad crossing, and then they were lost. The map led them to the wrong place, there wasn't anyone to ask for directions. Goner circled the sleepy streets, eventually stopped somewhere between a cemetery and a school stadium, got pissed, stepped out of the car, and lit up. Artem got out, too.

The stadium was unnerving. The cemetery was more fun. They listened to the wind, looked at the trees.

"I can't stand the end of summer," Goner said.

"How come?"

"Uh, it's kind of hopeless. Fall, school, adults. And you become more and more like them every year."

"Yeah, what a nightmare."

"Uh-huh."

"So what's the deal with this family?" Artem asked.

"Five kids. The oldest daughter is fifteen. They aren't sure how old the rest of them are. The parents are out of the picture. Some distant relatives called and asked me to drop some things off."

"Uh, what kind of lives do they have?"

"God only knows. Unhappy ones, probably."

"I see. How old are you?"

"Thirty-five," Goner replied, surprised. His age—that's the last thing anyone had asked him about lately.

"You've aged a lot over the last six months. It's like you were living on the streets."

"That would have been better," Goner said, throwing his cigarette butt out.

They hopped in the van and set out to look for them. Their house turned up on the next street over, behind a school. The road wasn't paved—a pile of broken bricks and construction garbage had simply been smoothed down. Their house turned out to be a crude two-story brick building. Insulating glass shone white and defiant on the two far windows on the first floor; the rest of the frames were old, unpainted. Plastic wrap covered several windows. The balconies were open and packed with junk. Antennas soared on the roof. No satellite dishes. Off to the side, stakes driven into the ground with laundry drying on them loomed; across the street from their house were thick, poisonous bushes which seemed to have simply frozen before engulfing everything here. Right under the windows, a table had been driven into the ground, and there was an ancient couch and several chairs next to it. In general, the whole building, the children's clothing out on the line, and the table with the couch next to it looked like decorations out of a play about unhappy love. You don't want to stick around after a play like that.

And there on the couch, in the chairs and stools, on each other's laps, sat children. Ten of them. Or twelve. There they sat, looking at these two outsiders.

Artem and Goner stopped, lowered the window, and looked, too, staying silent. Yet unlike the children, they had to get back, so Goner opened the door, heavily hopped onto the ground, walked around the van, and approached the children. Artem followed him.

"Dasha," Goner said.

Dasha sat in the center, the other, younger children huddled around her. She was tall, had dyed white hair, and wore a green T-shirt, light jeans, and pink sneakers. It was doubtful she had picked those clothes out, so they fit her like a uniform on a prisoner planning to escape. The rest of the children wore motley attire, too.

"Did you hold up a thrift store or something?" Goner asked. The children didn't answer. And Dasha remained silent. "So, are you Dasha?"

"Yeah."

"Are there any adults at home?"

"The adults are at work."

"Today's a national holiday," Goner said, reminding her.

"Can I take a message?" Dasha didn't bother arguing with him.

"We've brought some humanitarian aid. Kolia's friends asked us to. You know Kolia?"

"Nope."

"Where should we unload it?"

"You can unload it right here." Dasha stood up, shook the little ones off her lap, and walked away from the table toward them.

She stood there looking at Goner. Didn't offer to help. Eventually, Goner couldn't take it anymore; he went over to the van, opened the back door, and began emptying it. Artem helped. They grabbed the boxes and placed them at Dasha's feet. They unloaded everything, silent.

"There are some canned goods here," Goner said. Once again, he couldn't take it anymore. "There are different kinds of grains here. There's some children's food here. There are diapers here."

"What do we need diapers for?"

"I was told this was for children, so I brought diapers."

"Do you buy your children diapers, too?" Dasha asked.

"Do you want them or not?" Goner said, clearly losing his temper.

"Don't need them."

Goner silently grabbed the two boxes of diapers and fiercely flung them back into the van.

"That it?" he asked Dasha.

"Yeah," she replied.

"Are you going to look at what's in the boxes?"

"No. Thank you."

"Wait," Artem said. "We have to take a picture. For our report."

"Where should I stand?" Dasha asked.

"Right where you are."

She stood behind the boxes; the children surrounded her like the dwarves around Snow White. They took the picture and left.

They didn't talk on the way back, didn't feel like it.

"I still can't get used to this," Artem said. "The empty city. Children asking for canned food."

"They aren't asking for anything."

"Well, maybe that's the right thing to do."

"That's the right thing to do. Maybe."

"You know it is. There are things in life that are more important than canned goods."

"Like what?"

"Like your sense of dignity."

"Not everyone can pull off wearing clothes from a thrift store with a sense of dignity."

"They can."

Artem took out his phone and found the picture.

So youthful. So poor. The brick wall of a crude dwelling behind her, the busted doors of the apartment complexes surrounding her. The children's mocking and prickly gazes alongside her. She looks into the future and sees something there. Something you can't glimpse unless you're in her shoes. Something protracted, arduous, filled with pain, filled with joy. Something you can't share. Something you can't avoid. Something that isn't too pleasing. But it isn't anything to be scared of, either.

SERHIY ZHADAN was born in the Luhansk region of Ukraine and educated in Kharkiv, where he lives today. He is the most popular poet of the post-independence generation in Ukraine and the author of numerous books of poetry and prose, which have earned him national, continental, and international awards. His prose works include *Big Mac* (2003), *Depeche Mode* (2004), *Anarchy in the UKR* (2005), *Hymn of the Democratic Youth* (2006), *Voroshilovgrad* (2010), *Mesopotamia* (2014), and *The Orphanage* (2017), which won the 2022 European Bank for Reconstruction and Development Literature Prize. In 2022, Zhadan was awarded the Hannah Arendt Prize for Political Thought, as well as the Peace Prize of the German Book Trade for his "outstanding artistic work and his humanitarian stance with which he turns to the people suffering from war and helps them at the risk of his own life." He is the front man for the band Zhadan and the Dogs.

ISAAC STACKHOUSE WHEELER is a translator, poet, and educator from New Hampshire.

"Serhiy Zhadan is one of the most important writers of our time. These stories, which arise from his extraordinary engagement during Russia's war of atrocity against Ukraine, bring home both the reality of war and the necessity of literature."

—Timothy Snyder

The women, men, and children in Serhiy Zhadan's new collection of stories testify to the dignity of daily life in the war-battered Ukrainian city of Kharkiv. Through a series of powerful vignettes we witness the ordinary experiences of people in extraordinary times—weddings, love affairs, tense visits home from the battlefield, desperate deliveries of humanitarian aid.

Highlighting the upheaval since the 2022 Russian invasion, characters from Zhadan's *Mesopotamia* and *The Orphanage* reappear, this time with entirely different concerns: evacuating an elderly woman after the bombardment of a residential area; finding a job for someone who returned from the front with significant disabilities; attending the funeral of a colleague who had led a combat unit on the front lines.

These stories, composed shortly before the author joined the Ukrainian armed forces, give voice to the vulnerability of those whose lives have been transformed by war, who have come to accept that death lurks around every corner, in every building, and on every square.

"Certain writers become definitive: the standard against which others are measured. Zhadan is now that standard, not just for Ukraine but for world literature."

—Askold Melnyczuk

Serhiy Zhadan is an award-winning contemporary Ukrainian author of poetry and prose. His books include *The Orphanage*, *Sky Above Kharkiv*, and *How Fire Descends*.

Isaac Stackhouse Wheeler is a translator, poet, and educator from New Hampshire.

A MARGELLOS WORLD REPUBLIC OF LETTERS BOOK

For more information, visit yalebooks.com/margellos

Yale UNIVERSITY PRESS

New Haven and London

yalebooks.com yalebooks.co.uk

ISBN 978-0-300-28434-8